Kenneth
Barrett

MY SIDE
OF THE
MOUNTAIN

**Written and Illustrated by
JEAN GEORGE**

D0465644

SCHOLASTIC INC.
New York Toronto London Auckland Sydney Tokyo

ISBN 0-590-03425-1

35 34 33 32 31 30 29 28 27 26   4 5 6 7 8/8

Printed in the U. S. A.   01

CONTENTS

This book is dedicated
to many people

to that gang of youngsters who
inhabited the trees and waters of
the Potomac River so many years
ago, and to the bit of Sam Gribley
in the children and adults around
me now.

Gorge

tree house

Mountain meadow

Gribley Beech

apple tree

old house site

walnut tree

cattail supply

raft

My Side of the Mountain
signed S. Gribley

In Which I Hole Up
in a Snowstorm

"I AM ON MY MOUNTAIN in a tree home that people have passed without ever knowing that I am here. The house is a hemlock tree six feet in diameter, and must be as old as the mountain itself. I came upon it last summer, and dug and burned it out until I made a snug cave in the tree that I now call home.

"My bed is on the right as you enter, and is made of ash slats and covered with deerskin. On the left is a small fireplace about knee-high. It is of clay and stones. It has a chimney that leads the smoke out through a knothole. I chipped out three other knotholes to let fresh air in. The air coming in is bitter cold. It must be below zero outside, and yet I can sit here inside my tree and write with bare hands. The fire is small, too. It doesn't take much fire to warm this tree room.

"It is the fourth of December, I think. It may be the fifth. I am not sure because I have not recently counted the notches in the aspen pole that is my calendar. I have been just too busy gathering nuts and berries, smoking venison, fish, and small game to keep up with the exact date.

"The lamp I am writing by is deer fat poured into a turtle shell with a strip of my old city trousers for a wick.

"It snowed all day yesterday and today. I have not been outside since the storm began, and I am bored for the first time since I ran away from home eight months ago to live on the land.

"I am well and healthy. The food is good. Sometimes I eat turtle soup, and I know how to make acorn pancakes. I keep my supplies in the wall of the tree in wooden pockets that I chopped myself.

"Every time I have looked at those pockets during the last two days, I have felt just like a squirrel — which reminds me: I didn't see a squirrel one whole day before that storm began. I guess they are holed up and eating their stored nuts too.

"I wonder if The Baron — that's the wild weasel who lives behind the big boulder to the north of my tree — is also denned up. Well, anyway, I think the storm is dying down, because the tree is not crying so much. When the wind really blows, the whole tree moans right down to the roots, which is where I am.

"Tomorrow I hope The Baron and I can tunnel out into the sunlight. I wonder if I should dig the snow. But that would mean I would have to put it somewhere, and the only place to put it is in my nice snug tree. Maybe I can pack it with my hands as I go. I've always dug into the snow from the top — never up from under.

"The Baron must dig up from under the snow. I wonder where he puts what he digs. Well, I guess I'll know in the morning."

When I wrote that last winter, I was scared and thought maybe I'd never get out of my tree. I had been scared for two days — ever since the first blizzard hit the Catskill Mountains. When I came up to the sunlight, which I did by simply poking my head into the soft snow and standing up, I laughed at my dark fears.

Everything was white, clean, shining, and beautiful. The sky was blue, blue, blue. The hemlock grove was laced with snow, the meadow was smooth and white, and the gorge was sparkling with ice. It was so beautiful and peaceful that I laughed out loud. I guess I laughed because my first snowstorm was over and it had not been so terrible after all.

Then I shouted, "I did it!" My voice never got very far. It was hushed by the tons of snow.

I looked for signs from The Baron Weasel. His footsteps were all over the boulder — also slides where he had played. He must have been up for hours, enjoying the new snow.

Inspired by his fun, I poked my head into my tree and whistled. Frightful, my trained falcon, flew to my fist, and we jumped and slid down the mountain, making big holes and trenches as we went. It was good to be whistling and carefree again, because I was sure scared by the coming of that storm.

I had been working since May, learning how to make a fire with flint and steel, finding what plants I could eat, learning how to trap animals and catch fish — all this so that when the curtain of blizzard struck the Catskills, I could crawl inside my tree and be comfortably warm and have plenty to eat.

During the summer and fall I had thought about the coming of winter. However, on that third day of December when the sky blackened, the temperature dropped, and the first flakes swirled around me, I must admit that I wanted to run back to New York. Even the first night that I spent out in the woods, when I couldn't get the fire started, was not as frightening as the snowstorm that gathered behind the gorge and mushroomed up over my mountain.

I was smoking three trout. It was nine o'clock in the morning. I was busy keeping the flames low, so they would not leap up and burn the fish. As I worked, it occurred to me that it was awfully dark for that hour of the morning. Frightful was leashed to her tree stub. She seemed restless and pulled at her tethers. Then I realized that the forest was dead quiet. Even the woodpeckers that had been tapping around me all morning were silent. The squirrels were nowhere to be seen. The juncos and chickadees and nuthatches were gone. I looked to see what The Baron Weasel was doing. He was not around. I looked up.

From my tree you can see the gorge beyond the meadow. White water pours between the black wet boulders and cascades into the valley below. The water that day was as dark as the rocks. Only the sound told me it was still falling. Above the darkness stood another darkness — the clouds of winter, black and fearsome. They looked as wild as the winds that were bringing them. I grew sick with fright. I knew I had enough food. I knew everything was going to be perfectly all right. But knowing that didn't help. I was scared. I stamped out the fire and pocketed the fish.

I tried to whistle for Frightful, but couldn't purse my shaking lips tight enough to get out anything but *pfffff*. So I grabbed her by the hide straps that are attached to her legs and we dove through the deerskin door into my room in the tree.

I put Frightful on the bedpost and curled up in a ball on the bed. I thought about New York and the noise and the lights, and how a snowstorm always seemed very friendly there. I thought about our apartment, too. At that moment it seemed bright and lighted and warm. I had to keep saying to myself: there were eleven of us in it! Dad, Mother, four sisters, four brothers, and me. And not one of us liked it, except perhaps little Nina, who was too young to know. Dad didn't like it even a little bit. He had been a sailor once, but when I was born he gave up the sea and worked on the docks in New York. Dad didn't like the land. He liked the sea, wet and big and endless.

Sometimes he would tell me about Great-grandfather Gribley, who owned land in the Catskill Mountains and felled the trees and built a home and plowed the land — only to discover that he wanted to be a sailor. The farm failed, and Great-grandfather Gribley went to sea.

As I lay with my face buried in the sweet greasy smell of my deerskin, I could hear Dad's voice saying, "That land is still in the family's name. Somewhere in the Catskills is an old beech with the name *Gribley* carved on it. It marks the northern boundary of Gribley's folly — the land is no place for a Gribley."

"The land is no place for a Gribley," I said. "The land is no place for a Gribley, and here I am three hundred feet from the beech with *Gribley* carved on it."

I fell asleep at that point, and when I awoke I was hungry. I cracked some walnuts, got down the acorn flour I had pounded, with a bit of ash to remove the bite, reached out the door for a little snow, and stirred up some acorn pancakes. I cooked them on a top of a tin can, and as I ate them, smothered with blueberry jam, I knew that the land was just the place for a Gribley.

In Which I Get Started
on This Venture

I LEFT NEW YORK in May. I had a penknife, a ball of cord, an ax, and forty dollars, which I had saved from selling magazine subscriptions. I also had some flint and steel, which I had bought at a Chinese store in the city. The man in the store had showed me how to use it. He had also given me a little purse to put it in, and some tinder to catch the sparks. He had told me that if I ran out of tinder, I should burn cloth and use the charred ashes.

I thanked him and said, "This is the kind of thing I am not going to forget."

On the train north to the Catskills, I unwrapped my flint and steel and practiced hitting them together to make sparks. On the wrapping paper I made these notes:

"A hard brisk strike is best. Remember to hold the steel in the left hand and the flint in the right, and hit the steel with the flint.

"The trouble is the sparks go every which way."

And that *was* the trouble. I did not get a fire going that night, and as I mentioned, this was a scary experience.

I hitched rides into the Catskill Mountains. At about four o'clock a truck driver and I passed through a beautiful dark hemlock forest, and I said to him, "This is as far as I am going."

He looked all around and said, "You live here?"

"No," I said, "but I am running away from home, and this is just the kind of forest I have always dreamed I would run to. I think I'll camp here tonight." I hopped out of the cab.

"Hey, boy," the driver shouted. "Are you serious?"

"Sure," I said.

"Well, now, ain't that sumpin'? You know,

when I was your age, I did the same thing. Only thing was, I was a farm boy and ran to the city, and you're a city boy running to the woods. I was scared of the city — do you think you'll be scared of the woods?"

"Heck, no!" I shouted loudly.

As I marched into the cool shadowy woods, I heard the driver call to me, "I'll be back in the morning, if you want to ride home."

He laughed. Everybody laughed at me. Even Dad. I told Dad that I was going to run away to Great-grandfather Gribley's land. He had roared with laughter and told me about the time he had run away from home. He got on a boat headed for Singapore, but when the whistle blew for departure, he was down the gangplank and home in bed before anyone knew he was gone. Then he told me, "Sure, go try it. Every boy should try it."

I must have walked a mile into the woods until I found a stream. It was a clear, athletic stream that rushed and ran and jumped and splashed. Ferns grew along its bank, and its rocks were upholstered with moss.

I sat down, smelled the piney air, and took out my penknife. I cut off a green twig and began to whittle. I have always been good at whittling. I carved a ship once that my teacher exhibited for parents' night at school.

First I whittled an angle on one end of the twig. Then I cut a smaller twig and sharpened it to a point. I whittled an angle on that twig, and bound the two angles face to face with a strip of green bark. It was supposed to be a fishhook.

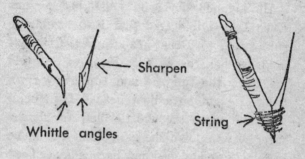

Wooden fish hook

According to a book on how to survive on the land that I read in the New York Public Library, this was the way to make your own hooks. I then dug for worms. I had hardly chopped the moss away with my ax before I hit frost. It had not occurred to me that there would be frost in the ground in May, but then I had not been on a mountain before.

This did worry me, because I was depending on fish to keep me alive until I got to my great-grandfather's mountain, where I was going to make traps and catch game.

I looked into the stream to see what else I could eat, and as I did, my hand knocked a rotten log apart. I remembered about old logs and all the sleeping stages of insects that are in it. I chopped away until I found a cold white grub.

I swiftly tied a string to my hook, put the grub on, and walked up the stream looking for a good place to fish. All the manuals I had read were very emphatic about where fish lived, and so I had memorized this: "In streams, fish usually congregate in pools and deep calm water. The heads of riffles, small rapids, the tail of a pool, eddies below rocks or logs, deep undercut banks, in the shade of overhanging bushes — all are very likely places to fish."

This stream did not seem to have any calm water, and I must have walked a thousand miles before I found a pool by a deep undercut bank in the shade of overhanging bushes. Actually, it wasn't that far; it just seemed that way because as I went looking and finding nothing, I was sure I was going to starve to death.

I squatted on this bank and dropped in my

19

line. I did so want to catch a fish. One fish would set me upon my way, because I had read how much you can learn from one fish. By examining the contents of its stomach, you can find what the other fish are eating or you can use the internal organs as bait.

The grub went down to the bottom of the stream. It swirled around and hung still. Suddenly the string came to life, and rode back and forth and around in a circle. I pulled with a powerful jerk. The hook came apart, and whatever I had went circling back to its bed.

Well, that almost made me cry. My bait was gone, my hook was broken, and I was getting cold, frightened, and mad. I whittled another hook, but this time I cheated and used string to wind it together instead of bark. I walked back to the log and luckily found another grub. I hurried to the pool, and I flipped a trout out of the water before I knew I had a bite.

The fish flopped, and I threw my whole body over it. I could not bear to think of it flopping itself back into the stream.

I cleaned it like I had seen the man at the fish market do, examined its stomach, and found it empty. This horrified me. What I didn't know was that an empty stomach means the fish are hungry and will eat about anything. However, I thought at the time that I was a goner. Sadly, I put some of the internal organs on my hook, and before I could get my line to the bottom I had another bite. I lost that one, but got the next one. I stopped when I had five nice little trout, and looked around for a place to build a camp and make a fire.

It wasn't hard to find a pretty spot along that stream. I selected a place beside a mossy rock in a circle of hemlocks.

I decided to make a bed before I cooked. I cut off some boughs for a mattress; then I leaned some dead limbs against the boulder and covered them with hemlock limbs. This made a kind of tent. I crawled in, lay down, and felt alone and secret and very excited.

But ah, the rest of this story! I was on the northeast side of the mountain. It grew dark and cold early. Seeing the shadows slide down on me, I frantically ran around gathering firewood. This is about the only thing I did right from that moment until dawn, because I remembered that the driest wood in a forest is the dead limbs that are still on the trees, and I gathered an enormous pile of them. That pile must still be there, for I never got a fire going.

I got sparks, sparks, sparks. I even hit the tinder with the sparks. The tinder burned

A couple of good shelters.
Make sure your fire is on scraped earth.
Also be sure to put it out!

all right, but that was as far as I got. I blew on it, I breathed on it, I cupped it in my hands; but no sooner did I add twigs than the whole thing went black.

Then it got too dark to see. I clicked steel and flint together, even though I couldn't see the tinder. Finally I gave up and crawled into my hemlock tent, hungry, cold, and miserable.

I can talk about that first night now, although it is still embarrassing to me because I was so stupid and scared that I hate to admit it.

I had made my hemlock bed right in the stream valley where the wind drained down from the cold mountaintop. It might have been all right if I had made it on the other side of the boulder, but I didn't. I was right on the main highway of the cold winds as they tore down upon the valley below. I didn't have enough hemlock boughs under me, and before I had my head down, my stomach was cold and damp. I took some boughs off the roof and stuffed them under me; and then my shoulders were cold. I curled up in a ball and was almost asleep when a whippoorwill called. If you have ever been within forty feet of a whippoorwill, you will understand why I couldn't even shut my eyes. They are deafening!

Well, anyway, the whole night went like that. I don't think I slept fifteen minutes, and I was so scared and tired that my throat was dry. I wanted a drink, but didn't dare go near the stream for fear of making a mis-step and falling in and getting wet. So I sat tight, and shivered and shook — and now I am able to say — I cried a little tiny bit.

Fortunately, the sun has a wonderfully glorious habit of rising every morning. When the sky lightened, when the birds awoke, I knew I would never again see anything so splendid as the round red sun coming up over the earth.

I was immediately cheered, and set out directly for the highway. Somehow I thought that if I was a little nearer the road, everything would be all right.

I climbed a hill and stopped. There was a house. A house, warm and cozy, with smoke coming out the chimney and lights in the windows, and only a hundred feet from my torture camp.

Without considering my pride, I ran down the hill and banged on the door. A nice old man answered. I told him everything in one long sentence, and then said, "And so, can I cook my fish here, because I haven't eaten in years?"

He chuckled, stroked his whiskery face, and

took the fish. He had them cooking in a pan before I knew what his name was.

When I asked him, he said Bill something; but I never heard his last name, because I fell asleep in his rocking chair that was pulled up beside his big hot glorious wood stove in the kitchen.

I ate the fish some hours later, also some bread, jelly, oatmeal, and cream. Then he said to me, "Sam Gribley, if you are going to run off and live in the woods, you better learn how to make a fire. Come with me."

We spent the afternoon practicing. I penciled these notes on the back of a scrap of paper, so I wouldn't forget:

"When the tinder glows, keep blowing and add fine dry needles one by one — and keep blowing, steadily, lightly, and evenly. Add one-inch dry twigs to the needles, and then give her a good big handful of small dry stuff. Keep blowing."

In Which I Find
Gribley's Farm

THE NEXT DAY I told Bill good-bye, and as I strode, warm and fed, onto the road, he called to me, "I'll see you tonight. The back door will be open if you want a roof over your head."

I said, "Okay," but I knew I wouldn't see Bill again. I knew how to make fire, and that was my weapon. With fire I could conquer the Catskills. I also knew how to fish. To fish and to make a fire: that was all I needed to know — I thought.

Three rides that morning took me to Delhi. Somewhere around here was Great-grandfather's beech tree with the name *Gribley* carved on it. This much I knew from Dad's stories.

By six o'clock I still had not found anyone who had even heard of the Gribleys, much less Gribley's beech, and so I slept on the porch of a schoolhouse and ate chocolate bars for supper. It was cold and hard, but I was so tired I could have slept in a wind tunnel.

At dawn I thought real hard: where would I find out about the Gribley farm? Some old map, I said. Where would I find an old map? The library? Maybe. I'd try it and see.

The librarian was very helpful. She was sort of young, had brown hair and brown eyes, and loved books as much as I did.

The library didn't open until ten thirty. I got there at nine. After I had lolled and rolled and sat on the steps for fifteen or twenty minutes, the door whisked open, and this tall lady asked me to come on in and browse around until opening time.

All I said to her was that I wanted to find the old Gribley farm, and that the Gribleys hadn't lived on it for maybe a hundred years, and she was off. I can still hear her heels click, when I think of her, scattering herself around those shelves finding me old maps, histories of the Catskills, and files of letters and deeds that must have come from attics around Delhi.

Miss Turner — that was her name — found it. She found Gribley's farm in an old book of Delaware County. Then she worked out the roads to it, and drew me maps and everything. Finally she said, "What do you want to know for? Some school project?"

"Oh no, Miss Turner, I want to go live there."

"But, Sam, it is all forest and trees now. The house is probably only a foundation covered with moss."

"That's just what I want. I am going to trap animals, and eat nuts and bulbs and berries, and make myself a house. You see, I am Sam Gribley, and I thought I would like to live on my great-grandfather's farm."

Miss Turner was the only person that believed me. She smiled, sat back in her chair, and said, "Well, I declare."

The library was just opening when I gathered the notes we had made and started off. As I pushed open the door, Miss Turner leaned over and said to me, "Sam, we have some very good books on plants and trees and animals, in case you get stuck."

I knew what she was thinking, and so I told her I would remember that.

With Miss Turner's map, I found the first stone wall that marked the farm. The old roads to it were all grown up and mostly gone, but by locating the stream at the bottom of the mountain I was able to begin at the bridge and go north and up a mile and a half. There, caterpillaring around boulders, roller-coasting up ravines and down hills, was the mound of rocks that had once been Great-grandfather's boundary fence.

And then, do you know, I couldn't believe I was there. I sat on the old gray stones a long time, looking through the forest, up that steep mountain, and saying to myself, "It must be Sunday afternoon, and it's raining; and Dad is trying to keep us all quiet by telling us about Great-grandfather's farm, and he's telling it so real that I can see it."

And then I said, "No. I am here, because I was never this hungry before."

I wanted to run all the way back to the library and tell Miss Turner that I had found it. Partly because she would have liked to have known and partly because Dad had said to me as I left, "If you find the place, tell someone at Delhi. I may visit you someday." Of course he was kidding, because he thought I'd be home the next day, but after many weeks maybe he would think I meant what I said, and he might come to see me.

However, I was too hungry to run back. I took my hook and line and went back down the mountain to the stream.

I caught a big old catfish. I climbed back to the stone wall in great spirits.

It was getting late, and so I didn't try to explore. I went right to work making a fire. I decided that even if I didn't have enough time to cut boughs for a bed, I was going to have cooked fish and a fire to huddle around during those cold night hours. May is not exactly warm in the Catskills.

By firelight that night I wrote this:

"Dear Bill [that was the old man] :

"After three tries I finally got a handful of dry grass on the glow in the tinder. Grass is even better than pine needles, and tomorrow I am going to try the outside bark of the river birch. I read somewhere that it has combustible oil in it that the Indians used to start fires. Anyway, I did just what you showed me, and had cooked catfish for dinner. It was good.

Your friend,
Sam."

After I wrote that, I remembered I didn't know his last name; and so I stuffed the note in my pocket, made myself a bed of boughs and leaves in the shelter of the stone wall, and fell right to sleep.

I must say this now about that first fire. It was magic. Out of dead tinder and grass and sticks came a live, warm light. It cracked and snapped and smoked and filled the woods with brightness. It lighted the trees and made them warm and friendly. It stood tall and bright and held back the night. Oh, this was a different night from the first dark frightful one. Also I was stuffed on catfish. I have since learned to cook it more, but never have I enjoyed a meal as much as that one, and never have I felt so independent again.

In Which I Find
Many Useful Plants

THE FOLLOWING MORNING I stood up, stretched and looked about me. Birds were dripping from the trees — little birds, singing and flying and pouring over the limbs.

"This must be the warbler migration," I said, and I laughed because there were so many birds. I had never seen so many. My big voice rolled through the woods, and their little voices seemed to rise and answer me.

They were eating. Three or four in a maple tree near me were darting along the limbs, pecking and snatching at something delicious on the trees. I wondered if there was anything there for a hungry boy. I pulled a limb down, and all I saw were leaves, twigs, and flowers. I ate a flower. It was not very good. One manual I had read said to watch what the birds and animals were eating in order to learn what is edible and non-edible in the forest. If the animal life can eat it, it is safe for humans. The book did suggest that a raccoon had tastes more nearly like ours. Certainly the birds were no example.

Then I wondered if they were not eating something I couldn't see — tiny insects perhaps. Well anyway, whatever it was, I decided to fish. I took my line and hook and walked down to the stream.

I lay on a log and dangled my line in the bright water. The fish were not biting. That made me hungrier. My stomach pinched. You know, it really does hurt to be terribly hungry.

A stream is supposed to be full of food. It is the easiest place to get a lot of food in a hurry. I needed something in a hurry, but what? I looked through the clear water and saw the tracks of mussels in the mud. I ran along the log back to shore, took off my clothes, and plunged into that icy water.

I collected almost a peck of mussels in very

little time at all, and began tying them in my
sweater to carry them back to camp.

"But I don't have to carry them anywhere," I said to myself. "I have my fire in
my pocket, I don't need a table. I can sit right
here by the stream and eat." And so I did. I
wrapped the mussels in leaves and sort of
steamed them in coals. They are not quite as
good as clams — a little stronger, I would
say — but by the time I had eaten three, I
had forgotten what clams tasted like and
knew only how delicious fresh-water mussels
were. I actually got full.

I wandered back to Great-grandfather's
farm and began to explore. Most of the acre-
age was maple and beech; some pine, dog-
woods, ash; and here and there a glorious
hickory. I made a sketch of the farm on my
road map, and put x's where the hickories
were. They were gold trees to me. I would
have hickory nuts in the fall. I could also
make salt from hickory limbs. I cut off one
and chopped it into bits and scraps. I stuck
them in my sweater.

The land was up and down and up and
down, and I wondered how Great-grandfather ever cut it and plowed it. There was one
stream running through it, which I was glad

to see, for it meant I did not have to go all the way down the mountain to the big creek for fish and water.

Around noon I came upon what I was sure was the old foundation of the house. Miss Turner was right. It was ruins — a few stones in a square, a slight depression for the basement, and trees growing right up through what had once been the living room. I wandered around to see what was left of the Gribley home.

After a few looks I saw an apple tree. I rushed up to it, hoping to find an old apple. No apples beneath it. About forty feet away, however, I found a dried one in the crotch of a tree, stuck there by a squirrel and forgotten. I ate it. It was pretty bad — but nourishing, I hoped. There was another apple tree and three walnuts. I scribbled x's. These were wonderful finds.

I poked around the foundations, hoping to uncover some old iron implements that I could use. I found nothing. Too many leaves had fallen and turned to loam, too many plants had grown up and died down over the old home site. I decided to come back when I had made myself a shovel.

Whistling and looking for food and shelter, I went on up the mountain, following the stone walls, discovering many things about my property. I found a marsh. In it were cattails and arrow-leaf — good starchy foods.

At high noon I stepped onto a mountain meadow. An enormous boulder rose up in the center of it. At the top of the meadow was a fringe of white birch. There were maples and oaks to the west, and a hemlock forest to the right that pulled me right across the sweet grasses, into it.

Never, never have I seen such trees. They were giants — old, old giants. They must have begun when the world began.

I started walking around them. I couldn't hear myself step, so dense and damp were the needles. Great boulders covered with ferns and moss stood among them. They looked like pebbles beneath those trees.

Standing before the biggest and the oldest and the most kinglike of them all, I suddenly had an idea.

About the Old, Old Tree

I KNEW ENOUGH about the Catskill Mountains to know that when the summer came, they were covered with people. Although Great-grandfather's farm was somewhat remote, still hikers and campers and hunters and fishermen were sure to wander across it.

Therefore I wanted a house that could not be seen. People would want to take me back where I belonged if they found me.

I looked at that tree. Somehow I knew it was home, but I was not quite sure how it was home. The limbs were high and not right for a tree house. I could build a back extension around it, but that would look silly.

Slowly I circled the great trunk. Halfway around the whole plan became perfectly obvious. To the west, between two of the flanges of the tree that spread out to be roots, was a cavity. The heart of the tree was rotting away. I scraped at it with my hands; old, rotten insect-ridden dust came tumbling out. I dug on and on, using my ax from time to time as my excitement grew.

With much of the old rot out, I could crawl in the tree and sit cross-legged. Inside I felt as cozy as a turtle in its shell. I chopped and chopped until I was hungry and exhausted. I was now in the hard good wood, and chopping it out was work. I was afraid December would come before I got a hole big enough to lie in. So I sat down to think.

You know, those first days I just never planned right. I had the beginnings of a home, but not a bite to eat, and I had worked so hard that I could hardly move forward to find that bite. Furthermore, it was discouraging to feed that body of mine. It was never satisfied, and gathering food for it took time and got it hungrier. Trying to get a place to rest it took time and got it more tired, and I really felt I was going in circles, and wondered how primitive man ever had enough time and energy to stop hunting food and start thinking about fire and tools.

I left the tree and went across the meadow looking for food. I plunged into the woods beyond, and there I discovered the gorge and the white cascade splashing down the black rocks into the pool below.

I was hot and dirty. I scrambled down the rocks and slipped into the pool. It was so cold I yelled. But when I came out on the bank and put on my two pairs of trousers and three sweaters, which I thought was a better way to carry clothes than in a pack, I tingled and burned and felt coltish. I leapt up the bank, slipped, and my face went down in a patch of dogtooth violets.

You would know them anywhere after a few looks at them at the Botanical Gardens and in colored flower books. They are little yellow lilies on long slender stems, with oval leaves dappled with gray. But that's not all. They have wonderfully tasty bulbs. I was filling my pockets before I got up from my fall.

"I'll have a salad-type lunch," I said as I moved up the steep sides of the ravine. I discovered that as late as it was in the season, the spring beauties were still blooming in the cool pockets of the woods. They are all right raw, that is if you are as hungry as I was. They taste a little like lima beans. I ate these as I went on hunting food, feeling better and better, until I worked my way back to the meadow where the dandelions were blooming. Funny I hadn't noticed them earlier. Their greens are good, and so are their roots — a little strong and milky, but you get used to that.

A crow flew into the aspen grove without saying a word. The little I knew of crows from following them in Central Park, they always have something to say. But this bird was sneaking, obviously trying to be quiet. Birds are good food. Crow is certainly not the best, but I did not know that then, and I launched out to see where it was going. I had a vague plan to try to noose it. This is one kind of thing I wasted time on in those days when time was so important. However, this venture turned out all right, because I did not have to noose that bird.

I stepped into the woods, looked around, could not see the crow, but noticed a big stick nest in a scrabbly pine. I started to climb the tree. Off flew the crow. What made me keep on climbing in face of such discouragement, I don't know, but I did, and that noon I had crow eggs and wild salad for lunch.

At lunch I also solved the problem of carving out my tree. After a struggle, I made a fire. Then I sewed a big skunk-cabbage leaf into a cup with grass strands. I had read that you can boil water in a leaf, and ever since then I had been very anxious to see if this were true. It seems impossible, but it works. I boiled the eggs in a leaf. The water keeps the leaf wet, and although the top dries up and burns down to the water level, that's as

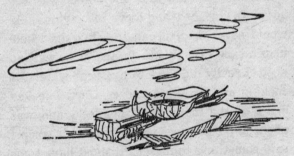

Good cooking fireplace with leaf bucket

far as the burning goes. I was pleased to see it work.

Then here's what happened. Naturally, all this took a lot of time, and I hadn't gotten very far on my tree, so I was fretting and stamping out the fire when I stopped with my foot in the air.

The fire! Indians made dugout canoes with fire. They burned them out, an easier and much faster way of getting results. I would try fire in the tree. If I was very careful, perhaps it would work. I ran into the hemlock forest with a burning stick and got a fire going inside the tree.

Thinking that I ought to have a bucket of water in case things got out of hand, I looked desperately around me. The water was far across the meadow and down the ravine. This would never do. I began to think the whole inspiration of a home in the tree was no good. I really did have to live near water for cooking and drinking and comfort. I looked sadly at the magnificent hemlock, and was about to put the fire out and desert it when I said something to myself. It must have come out of some book: "Hemlocks usually grow around mountain streams and springs."

I swirled on my heel. Nothing but boulders around me. But the air was damp, somewhere — I said — and darted around the rocks, peering and looking and sniffing and going down into pockets and dales. No water.

I was coming back, circling wide, when I almost fell in it. Two sentinel boulders, dripping wet, decorated with flowers, ferns, moss, weeds — everything that loved water — guarded a bathtub-sized spring.

"You pretty thing," I said, flopped on my stomach and pushed my face into it to drink. I opened my eyes. The water was like glass, and in it were little insects with oars. They rowed away from me. Beetles skittered like bullets on the surface, or carried a silver bubble of air with them to the bottom. Ha, then I saw a crayfish.

I jumped up, overturned rocks, and found many crayfish. At first I hesitated to grab them because they can pinch. I gritted my teeth, thought about how much more it hurts to be hungry, and came down upon them. I did get pinched, but I had my dinner. And that was the first time I had planned ahead! Any planning that I did in those early days was such a surprise to me and so successful that I was delighted with even a small plan. I wrapped the crayfish in leaves, stuffed them in my pockets, and went back to the burning tree.

Bucket of water, I thought. Bucket of water? Where was I going to get a bucket? How did I think, even if I found water, I could get it back to the tree? That's how citified I was in those days. I had never lived without a bucket before — scrub buckets, water buckets — and so when a water problem came up, I just thought I could run to the kitchen and get a bucket.

"Well, dirt is as good as water," I said as I ran back to my tree. "I can smother the fire with dirt."

Days passed working, burning, cutting, gathering food, and each day I cut another notch on an aspen pole that I had stuck in the ground for a calendar.

In Which I Meet
One of My Own Kind and Have
a Terrible Time Getting Away

FIVE NOTCHES INTO JUNE, my house was done. I could stand in it. lie down in it, and there was room left over for a stump to sit on. On warm evenings I would lie on my stomach and look out the door, listen to the cicadas and crickets, and hope it would storm so that I could crawl into my tree and be dry. I had gotten soaked during a couple of May downpours, and now that my house was done, I wanted the chance to sit in my hemlock and watch a cloudburst wet everything but me. This opportunity didn't come for a long time. It was dry.

One morning I was at the edge of the

meadow. I had cut down a small ash tree and was chopping it into lengths of about eighteen inches each. This was the beginning of my bed that I was planning to work on after supper every night.

With the golden summer upon me, food was much easier to get, and I actually had several hours of free time after supper in which to do other things. I had been eating frogs' legs, turtles, and best of all, an occasional rabbit. My snares and traps were set now. Furthermore, I had a good supply of cattail roots I had dug in the marsh.

If you ever eat cattails, be sure to cook them well; otherwise the fibers are tough and they take more chewing to get the starchy food from them than they are worth. However, they taste just like potatoes after you've been eating them a couple of weeks, and to my way of thinking are extremely good.

Well anyway, that summer morning when I was gathering material for a bed, I was singing and chopping and playing a game with a raccoon I had come to know. He had just crawled in a hollow tree and had gone to bed for the day when I came to the meadow. From time to time I would tap on his tree with my ax. He would hang his sleepy head

This device is set along an animal's runway.

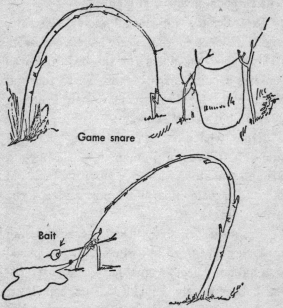

Game snare

Bait

This one will work sometimes, too.

out, snarl at me, close his eyes, and slide out of sight.

The third time I did this, I knew something was happening in the forest. Instead of closing his eyes, he pricked up his ears, and his face became drawn and tense. His eyes were focused on something down the mountain. I stood up and looked. I could see nothing. I squatted down and went back to work. The raccoon dove out of sight.

"Now what's got you all excited?" I said, and tried once more to see what he had seen.

I finished the posts for the bed, and was looking around for a bigger ash to fell and make slats for the springs when I nearly jumped out of my shoes.

"Now what are you doing up here all alone?" It was a human voice. I swung around and stood face to face with a little old lady in a pale blue sunbonnet and a loose brown dress.

"Oh gosh!" I said. "Don't scare me like that. Say one word at a time until I get used to a human voice." I must have looked frightened, because she chuckled, smoothed down the front of her dress, and whispered, "Are you lost?"

"Oh no, ma'am," I stuttered.

"Then a little fellow like you should not be all alone way up here on this haunted mountain."

"Haunted?" said I.

"Yes, indeed. There's an old story says

there are little men up here who play nine-pins right down in that gorge in the twi-light." She peered at me. "Are you one of them?"

"Oh no, no, no, no," I said. "I read that story. It's just make-believe." I laughed, and she puckered her forehead.

"Well, come on," she said, "make some use of yourself and help me fill this basket with strawberries."

I hesitated — she meant *my* strawberry supply.

"Now, get on with you. A boy your age should be doing something worth while, 'stead of playing mumbly peg with sticks. Come on, young man." She jogged me out into the meadow.

We worked quite a while before we said any more. Frankly, I was wondering how to save my precious, precious strawberries, and I may say I picked slowly. Each time I dropped one in her basket, I thought how good it would taste.

"Where do ye live?" I jumped. It is terri-bly odd to hear a voice after weeks of listen-ing only to birds and crickets and raccoons, and what is more, to hear the voice ask a question like that.

"I live here," I said.

"Ye mean Delhi. Fine. You can walk me home."

Nothing I added did any good. She would not be shaken from her belief that I lived in Delhi. So I let it go.

We must have reaped every last strawberry before she stood up, put her arm in mine, and escorted me down the mountain. I certainly was not escorting her. Her wiry little arms were like crayfish pinchers. I couldn't have gotten away if I had tried. So I walked and listened.

She told me all the local and world news, and it was rather pleasant to hear about the National League, an atom-bomb test, and a Mr. Riley's three-legged dog that chased her chickens. In the middle of all this chatter she said, "That's the best strawberry patch in the entire Catskill range. I come up here every spring. For forty years I've come to that meadow for my strawberries. It gits harder every year, but there's no jam can beat the jam from that mountain. I know. I've been around here all my life." Then she went right into the New York Yanks without putting in a period.

As I helped her across the stream on big boulders, I heard a cry in the sky. I looked up. Swinging down the valley on long pointed wings was a large bird. I was struck by the ease and swiftness of its flight.

"Duck hawk," she said. "Nest around here every year. My man used to shoot 'em. He said they killed chickens, but I don't believe it. The only thing that kills chickens is Mr. Riley's three-legged dog."

She tipped and teetered as she crossed the rocks, but kept right on talking and stepping as if she knew that no matter what, she would get across.

We finally reached the road. I wasn't listening to her very much. I was thinking about the duck hawk. This bird, I was sure, was the peregrine falcon, the king's hunting bird.

"I will get one. I will train it to hunt for me," I said to myself.

Finally I got the little lady to her brown house at the edge of town.

She turned fiercely upon me. I started back.

"Where are you going, young man?"

I stopped. Now, I thought, she is going to march me into town. Into town? "Well, that's where I'll go then," I said to myself. And I turned on my heel, smiled at her, and replied, "To the library."

The King's Provider

MISS TURNER was glad to see me. I told her I wanted some books on hawks and falcons, and she located a few, although there was not much to be had on the subject. We worked all afternoon, and I learned enough. I departed when the library closed. Miss Turner whispered to me as I left, "Sam, you need a haircut."

I hadn't seen myself in so long that this had not occurred to me. "Gee, I don't have any scissors."

She thought a minute, got out her library scissors, and sat me down on the back steps. She did a fine job, and I looked like any other boy who had played hard all day and who, with a little soap and water after supper, would be going off to bed in a regular house.

I didn't get back to my tree that night. The May apples were ripe, and I stuffed on those as I went through the woods. They taste like a very sweet banana, are earthy and a little slippery. But I liked them.

At the stream I caught a trout. Everybody thinks a trout is hard to catch because of all the fancy gear and flies and lines sold for trout fishing, but honestly, they are easier to catch than any other fish. They have big mouths, and snatch and swallow whole anything they see when they are hungry. With my wooden hook in its mouth, the trout was mine. The trouble is that trout are not hungry when most people have time to fish. I knew they were hungry that evening because the creek was swirling, and minnows and everything else were jumping out of the water. When you see that, go fish. You'll get them.

I made a fire on a flat boulder in the stream and cooked the trout. I did this so I could watch the sky. I wanted to see the falcon again. I also put the trout head on the hook and dropped it in the pool. A snapping turtle would view a trout head with relish.

I waited for the falcon patiently. I didn't have to go anywhere. After an hour or so, I was rewarded. A slender speck came from the valley and glided up the stream. It was still far away when it folded its wings and bombed the earth. I watched. It arose, clumsy and big — carrying food — and winged back to the valley.

I sprinted down the stream and made myself a lean-to near some cliffs where I thought the bird had disappeared. Having learned that day that duck hawks prefer to nest on cliffs, I settled for this site.

Early the next morning, I got up and dug the tubers of the arrow-leaf that grew along the stream bank. I baked these and boiled mussels for breakfast; then I curled up behind a willow and watched the cliff.

The hawks came in from behind me and circled the stream. They had apparently been out hunting before I had gotten up, as they were returning with food. This was exciting news. They were feeding young, and I was somewhere near the nest.

I watched one of them swing in to the cliff and disappear. A few minutes later it winged out empty-footed. I marked the spot mentally and said, "Ha!"

After splashing across the stream in the shallows, I stood at the bottom of the cliff and wondered how on earth I was going to climb the sheer wall.

I wanted a falcon so badly, however, that I dug in with my toes and hands and started up. The first part was easy; it was not too steep. When I thought I was stuck, I found a little ledge and shinnied up to it.

I was high, and when I looked down, the stream spun. I decided not to look down any more. I edged up to another ledge, and lay down on it to catch my breath. I was shaking from exertion and I was tired.

I looked up to see how much higher I had to go when my hand touched something moist. I pulled it back and saw that it was white — bird droppings. Then I saw them. Almost where my hand had been sat three fuzzy whitish-gray birds. Their wide-open mouths gave them a startled look.

"Oh hello, hello," I said. "You are cute."

When I spoke, all three blinked at once. All three heads turned and followed my hand as I swung it up and toward them. All three watched my hand with opened mouths. They were marvelous. I chuckled. But I couldn't reach them.

I wormed forward, and *wham!* — something hit my shoulder. It pained. I turned my head to see the big female. She had bit me. She winged out, banked, and started back for another strike.

Now I was scared, for I was sure she would cut me wide open. With sudden nerve, I stood up, stepped forward, and picked up the biggest of the nestlings. The females are bigger than the males. They are the "falcons." They are the pride of kings. I tucked her in my sweater and leaned against the cliff, facing the bulletlike dive of the falcon. I threw out my foot as she struck, and the sole of my tennis shoe took the blow.

The female was now gathering speed for another attack, and when I say speed, I mean fifty to sixty miles an hour. I could see myself battered and torn, lying in the valley below, and I said to myself, "Sam Gribley, you had better get down from here like a rabbit."

I jumped to the ledge below, found it was really quite wide, slid on the seat of my pants to the next ledge, and stopped. The hawk apparently couldn't count. She did not know I had a youngster, for she checked her nest, saw the open mouths, and then she forgot me.

I scrambled to the riverbed somehow, being very careful not to hurt the hot, fuzzy body that was against my own. However, Frightful, as I called her right then and there because of the difficulties we had had in getting together, did not think so gently of me. She dug her talons into my skin to brace herself during the bumpy ride to the ground.

I stumbled to the stream, placed her in a nest of buttercups, and dropped beside her. I fell asleep.

When I awoke, my eyes opened on two gray eyes in a white stroobly head. Small pinfeathers were sticking out of the stroobly down, like feathers in an Indian quiver. The big blue beak curled down in a snarl and up in a smile.

"Oh, Frightful," I said, "you are a raving beauty."

Frightful fluffed her nubby feathers and shook. I picked her up in the cup of my hands and held her under my chin. I stuck my nose in the deep warm fuzz. It smelled dusty and sweet.

I liked that bird. Oh, how I liked that bird from that smelly minute. It was so pleasant to feel the beating life and see the funny little awkward movements of a young thing.

The legs pushed out between my fingers, I gathered them up, together with the thrashing wings, and tucked the bird in one piece under my chin. I rocked.

"Frightful," I said, "you will enjoy what we are going to do."

I washed my bleeding shoulder in the creek, tucked the torn threads of my sweater back into the hole they had come out of, and set out for my tree.

A Brief Account of What
I Did About the First Man
Who Was After Me

AT THE EDGE OF THE MEADOW, I sensed all was not well at camp. How I knew there was a human being there was not clear to me then. I can only say that after living so long with the birds and animals, the movement of a human is like the difference between the explosion of a cap pistol and a cannon.

I wormed toward camp. When I could see the man I felt was there, I stopped and looked. He was wearing a forester's uniform. Immediately I thought they had sent someone out to bring me in, and I began to shake. Then I realized that I didn't have to go back to meet the man at all. I was perfectly free and capable of settling down anywhere. My tree was just a pleasant habit.

I circled the meadow and went over to the gorge. On the way I checked a trap. It was a deadfall. A figure four under a big rock. The rock was down. The food was rabbit.

I picked a comfortable place just below the rim of the gorge, where I could pop up every now and then and watch my tree. Here I dressed down the rabbit and fed Frightful some of the more savory bites from a young falcon's point of view: the liver, the heart, the brain. She ate in gulps. As I watched her swallow, I sensed a great pleasure. It is hard to explain my feelings at that moment. It seemed marvelous to see life pump through that strange little body of feathers, wordless noises, milk eyes — much as life pumped through me.

The food put the bird to sleep. I watched her eyelids close from the bottom up and her head quiver. The fuzzy body rocked, the tail spread to steady it, and the little duck hawk almost sighed as it sank into the leaves, sleeping.

I had lots of time. I was going to wait for the man to leave. So I stared at my bird, the beautiful details of the new feathers, the fernlike lashes along the lids, the saucy bristles at the base of the beak. Pleasant hours passed.

Frightful would awaken, I would feed her, she would fall back to sleep, and I would watch the breath rock her body ever so slightly. I was breathing the same way, only not so fast. Her heart beat much faster than mine. She was designed to her bones for a swifter life.

It finally occurred to me that I was very hungry. I stood up to see if the man were gone. He was yawning and pacing.

The sun was slanting on him now, and I could see him quite well. He was a fire warden. "Of course it has not rained," I told myself, "for almost three weeks, and the fire planes have been circling the mountains and valleys, patrolling the mountains." Apparently the smoke from my fire was spotted, and a man was sent to check it. I recalled the bare trampled ground around the tree, the fireplace of rocks filled with ashes, the wood chips from the making of my bed, and resolved hereafter to keep my yard clean.

So I made rabbit soup in a tin can I found at the bottom of the gorge. I seasoned it with wild garlic and jack-in-the-pulpit roots.

Jack-in-the-pulpits have three big leaves on a stalk and are easily recognized by the curly striped awning above a stiff, serious preacher named Jack. The jack-in-the-pulpits were acrid; they needed to be pounded to flour and allowed to stand, to be really good. I had to eat them bitter.

The fire I made was only of the driest wood, and I made it right at the water's edge. I didn't want a smoky fire on this particular evening.

After supper I made a bough bed and stretched out with Frightful beside me. Apparently, the more you stroke and handle a falcon, the easier they are to train.

I had all sorts of plans for hoods and jesses, as the straps on a falcon are called, and I soon forgot about the man.

Stretched on the boughs, I listened to the wood peewees calling their haunting good nights until I fell sound asleep.

In Which I Learn to Season My Food

THE FIRE WARDEN made a fire some time
in the colder hours of the night. At dawn he
was asleep beside white smoldering ashes. I
crawled back to the gorge, fed Frightful rabbit bites, and slipped back to the edge of the
meadow to check a box trap I had set the day
before. I made it by tying small sticks together like a log cabin. This trap was better
than the snares or deadfalls. It had caught
numerous rabbits, several squirrels, and a
groundhog.

I saw, as I inched toward it, that it was
closed. The sight of a closed trap excites me to
this day. I still can't believe that animals

don't understand why delicious food is in such a ridiculous spot.

Well, this morning I pulled the trap deep into the woods to open it. The trapped animal was light. I couldn't guess what it was. It was also active, flipping and darting from one corner to the next. I peeked in to locate it, so that I could grab it quickly behind the head without getting bitten. I was not always successful at this, and had scars to prove it.

I put my eye to the crack. A rumpus arose in the darkness. Two bright eyes shone, and out through that hole that was no wider than a string bean came a weasel. He flew right out at me, landed on my shoulder, gave me a lecture I shall never forget, and vanished under the scant cover of trillium and bloodroot leaves.

He popped up about five feet away and stood on his hind feet to lecture me again. I said, "Scat!" so he darted right to my knee, put his broad furry paws on my pants, and looked me in the face. I shall never forget the fear and wonder that I felt at the bravery of that weasel. He stood his ground and berated me. I could see by the flashing of his eyes and the curl of his lip that he was furious at me for trapping him. He couldn't talk, but I knew what he meant.

Wonder filled me as I realized he was absolutely unafraid. No other animal, and I knew quite a few by now, had been so brave in my presence. Screaming, he jumped on me. This surprised and scared me. He leapt from my lap to my head, took a mouthful of hair and wrestled it. My goose bumps rose. I was too frightened to move. A good thing too, because I guess he figured I was not going to fight back, and his scream of anger changed to a purr of peace. Still, I couldn't move.

Presently, down he climbed, as stately as royalty, and off he marched, never looking back. He sank beneath the leaves like a fish beneath the water. Not a stem rippled to mark his way.

And so The Baron and I met for the first time, and it was the beginning of a harassing but wonderful friendship.

Frightful had been watching all this. She was tense with fright. So young and inexperienced, but she knew an enemy when she saw one. I picked her up and whispered into her birdy-smelling neck feathers.

"You wild ones know."

Since I couldn't go home, I decided to spend

the day in the marsh down the west side of the mountain. There were a lot of cattails and frogs there.

Frightful balanced on my fist as we walked. She had learned that in the short span of one afternoon and a night. She is a very bright bird.

On our way we scared up a deer. It was a doe. I watched her dart gracefully away, and said to Frightful, "That's what I want. I need a door for my house, tethers for you, and a blanket for me. How am I going to get a deer?"

This was not the first time I had said this. The forest was full of deer, and I already had drawn plans on a piece of birch bark for deadfalls, pit traps, and snares. None seemed workable.

The day passed. In the early evening we stole home, tree by tree, to find that the warden had gone. I cleaned up my front yard, scattered needles over the bare spots, and started a small fire with very dry wood that would not smoke much. No more wardens for me. I liked my tree, and although I could live somewhere else, I certainly did not want to.

Once home, I immediately started to work again. I had a device I wanted to try, and put some hickory sticks in a tin can and set it to boiling while I fixed dinner. Before going to bed, I noted this on a piece of birch bark:

"This night I am making salt. I know that people in the early days got along without it, but I think some of these wild foods would taste better with some flavoring. I understand that hickory sticks, boiled dry, leave a salty residue. I am trying it."

In the morning I added:

"It is quite true. The can is dry, and thick with a black substance. It is very salty, and I tried it on frogs' legs for breakfast. It is just what I have needed."

And so I went into salt production for several days, and chipped out a niche inside the tree in which to store it.

"*June 19*

"I finished my bed today. The ash slats work very well, and are quite springy and comfortable. The bed just fits in the right-hand side of the tree. I have hemlock boughs on it now, but hope to have deer hide soon. I am making a figure-four trap as tall as me, with a log on it that I can barely lift. It doesn't look workable. I wish there was another way of getting a deer.

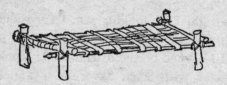

Bed made with ash slats

"June 20

"I decided today to dig a pit to trap a deer, so I am whittling a shovel out of a board I found in the stream this morning. That stream is very useful. It has given me tin cans for pots, and now an oaken board for a shovel.

"Frightful will hop from the stump to my fist. She still can't fly. Her wing feathers are only about an inch long. I think she likes me."

How a Door Came to Me

ONE MORNING before the wood peewees were up, I was smoking a mess of fish I had caught in the stream. When I caught more than I could eat, I would bone them, put them on a rack of sticks, and slowly smoke them until they dried out. This is the best way to preserve extra food. However, if you try it, remember to use a hard wood — hickory is the best. I tried pine on the first batch, and ruined them with black tarry smoke. Well, it was very silent — then came a scream. I jumped into my tree. Presently I had enough nerve to look out.

"Well, Baron Weasel!" I said in astonishment. I was sure it was the same weasel I had met in the trap. He was on the boulder in front of the hemlock, batting the ferns with his front feet and rearing and staring at me.

"Now, you stay right there," I said. Of course he flipped and came off the rock like a jet stream. He was at the door before I could stop him, and loping around my feet like a bouncing ball.

"You look glad all over, Baron. I hope all that frisking means joy," I said. He took my pants leg in his teeth, tugged it, and then rippled softly back to the boulder. He went down a small hole. He popped up again, bit a fern near by, and ran around the boulder. I crept out to look for him — no weasel. I poked a stick in the hole at the base of the rock, try-ing to provoke him, I felt a little jumpy, so that when a shot rang out through the woods I leapt a foot in the air and dove into my hole. A cricket chirped, a catbird scratched the leaves. I waited. One enormous minute later a dark form ran onto the meadow. It stumbled and fell.

I had the impression that it was a deer. Without waiting to consider what I might be running toward, I burst to the edge of the meadow.

No one was in sight, I ran into the grass. There lay a dead deer! With all my strength I dragged the heavy animal into the woods. I then hurried to my tree, gathered up the hemlock boughs on my bed, rushed back and threw them over the carcass. I stuck a few ferns in them so they would look as if they were growing there, and ran back to camp, breathless.

Hurriedly I put out the fire, covered it with dirt, hid my smoking rack in the spring, grabbed Frightful, and got in my tree.

Someone was poaching, and he might be along in a minute to collect his prize. The shot had come from the side of the mountain, and I figured I had about four minutes to clean up before the poacher arrived.

Then when I was hidden and ready, Frightful started her cry of hunger. I had not fed her yet that morning. Oh, how was I going to explain to her the awful need to be quiet? How did a mother falcon warn her young of danger? I took her in my hands and stroked her stomach. She fought me, and then she lay still in my hand, her feet up, her eyes bright. She stiffened and drooped. I kept on stroking her. She was hypnotized. I would stop for a few moments; she would lie still, then pop to her feet. I was sure this wasn't what her mother did to keep her quiet, but it worked.

Bushes cracked, leaves scuttled, and a man with a shotgun came into the meadow. I could just see his head and shoulders. He looked around and banged toward the hemlock forest. I crawled up on my bed and stroked the hungry Frightful.

I couldn't see the man from my bed, but I could hear him.

I heard him come to the tree. I could see his boots. He stopped by the ashes of the fire, and then went on. I could see my heart lift my sweater. I was terrified.

I stayed on the bed all morning, telling the fierce little bundle of feathers in my hand that there was deer meat in store for her if she would just wait with me.

Way down the other side of the mountain, I heard another shot. I sure hoped that deer dropped on the poacher's toes and that he would now go home.

At noon I went to my prize. Frightful sat beside me as I skinned and quartered it. She ate deer until she was misshapen.

I didn't make any notes as to how long it took me to do all the work that was required to get the deer ready for smoking, and the hide scraped and ready for tanning, but it was many, many days.

However, when I sat down to a venison steak, that was a meal! All it was, was venison. I wrote this on a piece of birch bark: "I think I grew an inch on venison!" Frightful and I went to the meadow when it was done, and I flopped in the grass. The stars came up, the ground smelled sweet, and I closed my eyes. I heard *Pip, pop, pop, pop*.

"Who's making that noise?" I said sleepily to Frightful. She ruffled her feathers.

I listened. *Pop, pip*. I rolled over and stuck my face in the grass. Something gleamed beneath me, and in the fading light I could see an earthworm coming out of its hole.

Nearby another one arose and there was a *pop*. Little bubbles of air snapped as these voiceless animals of the earth came to the surface. That got me to smiling. I was glad to know this about earthworms. I don't know why, but this seemed like one of the nicest things I had learned in the woods — that earthworms, lowly, confined to the darkness of the earth, could make just a little stir in the world.

In Which Frightful
Learns Her ABC's

FREE TIME WAS SPENT scraping the fur off
the deer hide to get it ready for tanning. This
much I knew: in order to tan hide, it has to
be steeped in tannic acid. There is tannic acid
in the woods in oak trees, but it took me several weeks to figure out how to get it. You
need a lot of oak chips in water. Water and
oak give off tannic acid. My problem was not
oak or water, but getting a vessel big enough
to put the deer hide in.

Coming home from the stream one night,
I had an inspiration.

It had showered the day before, and as
Frightful and I passed an old stump, I noticed that it had collected the rain. "A stump,
an oak stump, would be perfect," I said right
out loud to that pretty bird.

So I felled an oak over by the gorge, burned
a hole in it, carried water to it, and put

my deerskin in it. I let it steep, oh, maybe
five days before I took it out and dried it. It
dried stiff as a board, and I had to chew, rub,
jump on it, and twist it to get it soft. When
this was done, however, I had my door. I
hung it on pegs inside my entrance, and because it was bigger than it had to be, I would
cut off pieces now and then when I needed

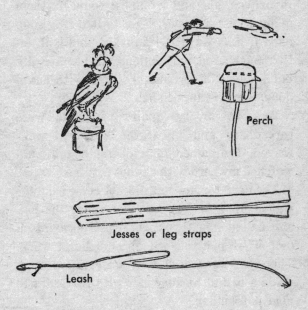

Perch

Jesses or leg straps

Leash

them. I cut off two thin strips to make jesses,
or leg straps, for Frightful. All good falcons
wear jesses and leashes so they can be tethered for their training.

I smoked the meat I couldn't eat and stored it. I used everything I could on that animal. I even used one of its bones for a spearhead. I was tired of catching frogs by the jump-and-miss system. I made two sharp points and strapped them to the end of a long stick, one on each side, to make a kind of fork. It worked beautifully. Frogs were one of my favorite meals, and I found I could fix them many ways; however, I got to like frog soup fixed in this way: "Clean, skin, and boil until tender. Add wild onions, also water lily bulbs and wild carrots. Thicken with acorn flour. Serve in turtle shell."

By now my two pairs of pants were threadbare and my three sweaters were frayed. I dreamed of a deerskin suit, and watched my herd with clothes in mind.

The deer for my suit did not come easily. I rigged up a figure-four trap under the log, and baited it with elderberries rolled into a ball. That just mushed up and didn't work. Then I remembered that deer like salt. I made a ball of hickory salt with turtle fat to hold it together.

Every evening Frightful and I, sometimes accompanied by The Baron Weasel, would go to the edge of the meadow and look toward the aspen grove to see if the great log had fallen. One night we saw three deer standing around it quietly, reaching toward the smell of salt. At that moment The Baron jumped at my pants leg, but got my ankle with an awful nip. I guess I had grown some; my pants and socks did not meet any more. I screamed, and the deer fled.

I chased The Baron home. I had the uneasy feeling that he was laughing as he darted, flipped, buckled, and disappeared.

The Baron was hard to understand. What did he want from me? Occasionally I left him bites of turtle or venison, and although he smelled the offerings, he never ate them. The catbird would get them. Most animals stick around if you feed them. But The Baron did not eat anything. Yet he seemed to like me. Gradually it occurred to me that he didn't have a mate or a family. Could he be a lonely bachelor, taking up with odd company for lack of an ordinary life? Well, whatever, The Baron liked me for what I was, and I appreciated that. He was a personable little fellow.

Every day I worked to train Frightful. It was a long process. I would put her on her stump with a long leash and step back a few feet with some meat in my hand. Then I would whistle. The whistle was supposed eventually to mean food to her. So I would whistle, show her the meat, and after many false flaps she would finally fly to my hand. I would pet her and feed her. She could fly fairly well, so now I made sure that she never ate unless she flew to my fist.

One day at breakfast I whistled for Frightful. I had no food, she wasn't even hungry, but she came to me anyway. I was thrilled. She had learned a whistle meant "come."

I looked into her steely eyes that morning and thought I saw a gentle recognition. She puffed up her feathers as she sat on my hand. I call this a "feather word." It means she is content.

Now each day I stepped farther and farther away from Frightful, to make her fly greater and greater distances. One day she flew a good fifty feet, and we packed up and went gathering seeds, bark, and tubers to celebrate.

I used my oldest sweater for gathering things. It was not very convenient, and each time I filled it I mentally designed bigger and better pockets on my deer-hide suit-to-be.

The summer was wonderful. There was food in abundance, and I gathered it most of the morning and stored it away in the afternoon. I could now see that my niches were not going to be big enough for the amount of food I would need for the winter, so I began burning out another tree. When the hickory nuts, walnuts, and acorns appeared, I was going to need a bin. You'd be surprised what a pile of nuts it takes to make one turtle shell full of nut meats — and not a snapping-turtle shell either, just a box-turtle shell!

With the easy living of the summer also came a threat. Hikers and vacationers were in the woods, and more than once I pulled inside my tree, closed my deer-flap door, and hid while bouncing noisy people crossed the meadow on their way to the gorge. Apparently the gorge was a sight for those who wanted a four-mile hike up the mountain.

One morning I heard a group arriving. I whistled for Frightful. She came promptly. We dove into the tree. It was dark in the tree with the flap closed, and I realized that I needed a candle. I planned a lamp of a turtle shell with a deer-hide wick, and as I was cutting off a piece of hide, I heard a shrill scream.

The voices of the hikers became louder. I wondered if one of them had fallen into the gorge. Then I said to Frightful, "That was no cry of a human, pretty bird. I'll bet you a rabbit for dinner that our deer trap worked. And here we are stored in a tree like a nut and unable to claim our prize."

We waited and waited until I couldn't be patient any more, and I was about to put my head out the door when a man's voice said, "Look at these trees!"

A woman spoke. "Harold, they're huge. How old do you think they are?"

"Three hundred years old, maybe four hundred," said Harold.

They tramped around, actually sat on The Baron's boulder, and were apparently going to have lunch when things began to happen out there and I almost gave myself away with hysterics.

"Harold, what's the matter with that weasel? It's running all over this rock." A scream! A scuttering and scraping of boots on the rocks.

"He's mad!" That was the woman.

"Watch it, Grace, he's coming at your feet." They ran.

By this time I had my hand over my mouth to keep back the laughter. I snorted and choked, but they never heard me. They were in the meadow — run right out of the forest by that fiery Baron Weasel.

I still laugh when I think of it.

It was not until dark that Frightful and I got to the deer, and a beauty it was.

The rest of June was spent smoking it, tanning it, and finally starting on my deer-skin suit. I made a bone needle, cut out the pants by riping up one pair of old city pants for a pattern. I saved my city pants and burned them bit by bit to make charred cloth for the flint and steel.

"Frightful," I said while sewing one afternoon. She was preening her now silver-gray, black, and white feathers. "There is no end to this. We need another deer. I can't make a blouse."

We didn't get another deer until fall, so with the scraps I made big square pockets for food gathering. One hung in front of me, and the other down my back. They were joined by straps. This device worked beautifully.

Sometime in July I finished my pants. They fit well, and were the best looking pants I had ever seen. I was terribly proud of them.

With pockets and good tough pants I was willing to pack home many more new foods to try — daisies, the bark of a poplar tree that I saw a squirrel eating, and puffballs. They are mushrooms, the only ones I felt were safe to eat, and even at that I kept waiting to die the first night I ate them. I didn't, so I enjoyed them from that night on. They are wonderful. Mushrooms are dangerous, and I would not suggest that one eat them from the forest. The mushroom expert at the Botanical Gardens told me that. He said even he didn't eat wild ones.

The inner bark of the poplar tree tasted like wheat kernels, and so I dried as much as I could and powdered it into flour. It was tedious work, and in August when the acorns were ready, I found that they made better flour and were much easier to handle.

I would bake the acorns in the fire, and grind them between stones. This was tedious work too, but now that I had a home and smoked venison and did not have to hunt food every minute, I could do things like make flour. I would simply add spring water to the flour and bake this on a piece of tin. When done, I had the best pancakes ever. They were flat and hard, like I imagined Indian bread to be. I liked them, and would carry the leftovers in my pockets for lunch.

One fine August day I took Frightful to the meadow. I had been training her to the lure. That is, I now tied her meat on a piece of wood, covered with hide and feathers. I would throw it in the air, and she would swoop out of the sky and catch it. She was absolutely free during these maneuvers, and would fly high into the air and hover over me like a leaf. I made sure she was very hungry before I turned her loose. I wanted her back.

After a few tries, she never missed the lure. Such marksmanship thrilled me. Bird and lure would drop to the earth, I would run over, grab her jesses, and we would sit on the big boulder in the meadow while she ate. Those were nice evenings. The finest was the night I wrote this:

"Frightful caught her first prey. She is now a trained falcon. It was only a sparrow, but we are on our way. It happened unexpectedly. Frightful was climbing into the sky, circling and waiting for the lure, when I stepped forward and scared a sparrow.

"The sparrow flew across the meadow. Out of the sky came a black streak — I've never seen anything drop so fast. With a great backwatering of wings, Frightful broke her fall, and at the same time seized the sparrow. I took it away from her and gave her the lure. That sounds mean, but if she gets in the habit of eating what she catches, she will go wild."

In Which I Find a
Real Live Man

ONE OF THE GASPING JOYS of summer was my daily bath in the spring. It was cold water. I never stayed in long, but it woke me up and started me into the day with a vengeance.

I would tether Frightful to a hemlock bough above me and splash her from time to time. She would suck in her chest, look startled, and then shake. While I bathed and washed, she preened. Huddled down in the water between the ferns and moss, I scrubbed myself with the bark of the slippery elm. It gets soapy when you rub it.

The frogs would hop out and let me in, and the woodthrush would come to the edge of the pool to see what was happening. We were a gay gathering — me shouting, Frightful preening, the woodthrush cocking its pretty head. Occasionally The Baron Weasel would pop up and glance furtively at us. He didn't care for water. How he stayed glossy and clean was a mystery to me, until he came to the boulder beside our bath pool one day, wet with the dew from the ferns. He licked himself until he was polished.

One morning there was a rustle in the leaves above. Instantly, Frightful had it located. I had learned to look where Frightful looked when there were disturbances in the forest. She always saw life before I could focus my eyes. She was peering into the hemlock above us. Finally I too saw it. A young raccoon. It was chittering, and now that all eyes were upon it, began coming down the tree.

And so Frightful and I met Jessie Coon James, the bandit of the Gribley farm.

He came headfirst down to our private bath, a scrabbly skinny young raccoon. He must have been from a late litter, for he was not very big and certainly not well fed. Whatever had been Jessie C. James's past, it was awful. Perhaps he was an orphan, perhaps he had been thrown out of his home by his mother, as his eyes were somewhat crossed and looked a little peculiar. In any event he had come to us for help, I thought, and so Frightful and I led him home and fed him.

In about a week he fattened up. His crumply hair smoothed out, and with a little ear scratching and back rubbing, Jessie C. James became a devoted friend. He also became useful. He slept somewhere in the dark tops of the hemlocks all day long, unless he saw us start for the stream. Then, tree by tree, limb by limb, Jessie followed us. At the stream he was the most useful mussel digger that any boy could have. Jessie could find mussels where three men could not. He would start to eat them; and if he ate them, he got full and wouldn't dig any more, so I took them away from him until he found me all I wanted. Then I let him have some.

Mussels are good. Here are a few notes on how to fix them:

"Scrub mussels in spring water. Dump them into boiling water with salt. Boil five minutes. Remove and cool in the juice. Take out meat. Eat by dipping in acorn paste flavored with a smudge of garlic and green apples."

Frightful took care of the small-game supply, and now that she was an expert hunter we had rabbit stew, pheasant potpie, and an occasional sparrow, which I generously gave to Frightful. As fast as we removed the rabbits and pheasants, new ones replaced them.

Beverages during the hot summer became my chore, largely because no one else wanted them. I found some sassafras trees at the edge of the road one day, dug up a good supply of roots, peeled and dried them. Sassafras tea is about as good as anything you want to drink. Pennyroyal makes another good drink. I dried great bunches of this, and hung them from the roof of the tree room together with the leaves of winterberry. All these fragrant plants I also used in cooking to give a new taste to some not-so-good foods.

The room in the tree smelled of smoke and mint. It was the best-smelling tree in the Catskill Mountains.

Life was leisurely. I was warm, well fed. One day while I was down the mountain, I returned home by way of the old farmhouse site to check the apple crop. They were summer apples, and were about ready to be picked. I had gathered a pouchful and had sat down under the tree to eat a few and think about how I would dry them for use in the winter when Frightful dug her talons into my shoulder so hard I winced.

"Be gentle, bird!" I said to her.

I got her talons out and put her on a log, where I watched her with some alarm. She was as alert as a high-tension wire, her head cocked so that her ears, just membranes under her feathers, were pointed east. She evidently heard a sound that pained her. She opened her beak. Whatever it was, I could hear nothing, though I strained my ears, cupped them, and wished she would speak.

Frightful was my ears as well as my eyes. She could hear things long before I. When she grew tense, I listened or looked. She was scared this time. She turned round and round on the log, looked up in the tree for a perch, lifted her wings to fly, and then stood still and listened.

Then I heard it. A police siren sounded far down the road. The sound grew louder and louder, and I grew afraid. Then I said, "No, Frightful, if they are after me there won't be a siren. They'll just slip up on me quietly."

No sooner had I said this than the siren wound down and apparently stopped on the road at the foot of the mountain. I got up to run to my tree, but had not gotten past the walnut before the patrol cars started up and screamed away.

We started home, although it was not late in the afternoon. However, it was hot, and thunderheads were building up. I decided to take a swim in the spring and work on the moccasins I had cut out several days ago.

With the squad car still on my mind, we slipped quietly into the hemlock forest. Once again Frightful almost sent me through the crown of the forest by digging her talons into my shoulder. I looked at her. She was staring at our home. I looked too. Then I stopped, for I could make out the form of a man stretched between the sleeping house and the store tree.

Softly, tree by tree, Frightful and I approached him. The man was asleep. I could have left and camped in the gorge again, but my enormous desire to see another human being overcame my fear of being discovered.

We stood above the man. He did not move, so Frightful lost interest in my fellow being. She tried to hop to her stump and preen. I grabbed her leash however, as I wanted to think before awakening him. Frightful flapped. I held her wings to her body, as her flapping was noisy to me. Apparently not so to the man. The man did not stir. It is hard to realize that the rustle of a falcon's wings is not much of a noise to a man from the city, because by now one beat of her wings and I would awaken from a sound sleep as if a shot had gone off. The stranger slept on. I realized how long I'd been in the mountains.

Right at that moment, as I looked into his unshaven face, his close-cropped hair, and his torn clothes, I thought of the police siren and put two and two together.

"An outlaw!" I said to myself. "Wow!" I had to think what to do with an outlaw before I awoke him.

Would he be troublesome? Would he be mean? Should I go live in the gorge until he moved on? How I wanted to hear his voice, to tell him about The Baron and Jessie C. James, to say words out loud. I really did not want to hide from him; besides, he might be hungry, I thought. Finally I spoke.

"Hi!" I said. I was delighted to see him roll over, open his eyes and look up. He seemed startled, so I reassured him. "It's all right, they've gone. If you don't tell on me, I won't tell on you." When he heard this, he sat up and seemed to relax.

"Oh," he said. Then he leaned against the tree and added, "Thanks." He evidently was thinking this over, for he propped his head on his elbow and studied me closely.

"You're a sight for sore eyes," he said, and smiled. He had a nice smile — in fact, he looked nice and not like an outlaw at all. His eyes were very blue, and although tired, they did not look scared or hunted.

However, I talked quickly before he could get up and run away.

"I don't know anything about you, and I don't want to. You don't know anything about me and don't want to, but you may stay here if you like. No one is going to find you here. Would you like some supper?" It was still early, but he looked hungry.

"Do you have some?"

"Yes, venison or rabbit?"

"Well . . . venison." His eyebrows puckered in question marks. I went to work.

He arose, turned around and around, and looked at his surroundings. He whistled softly when I kindled a spark with the flint and steel. I was now quite quick at this, and had a tidy fire blazing in a very few minutes. I was so used to myself doing this that it had not occurred to me that it would be interesting to a stranger.

"Desdemondia!" he said. I judged this to be some underworld phrase. At this moment

Frightful, who had been sitting quietly on her stump, began to preen. The outlaw jumped back, then saw she was tied and said, "And who is this ferocious looking character?"

"That is Frightful. Don't be afraid — she's quite wonderful and gentle. She would be glad to catch you a rabbit for supper if you would prefer that to venison."

"Am I dreaming?" said the man. "I go to sleep by a campfire that looked like it was built by a Boy Scout, and I awaken in the middle of the eighteenth century."

I crawled into the store tree to get the smoked venison and some cattail tubers. When I came out again, he was speechless.

"My storehouse," I explained.

"I see," he answered. From that moment on he did not talk much. He just watched me. I was so busy cooking the best meal that I could possibly get together that I didn't say much either. Later I wrote down that menu, as it was excellent.

"Brown puffballs in deer fat with a little wild garlic, fill pot with water, put venison in, boil. Wrap tubers in leaves and stick in coals. Cut up apples and boil in can with dogtooth violet bulbs. Raspberries to finish meal."

When the meal was ready, I served it to the man in my nicest turtle shell. I had to whittle him a fork out of the crotch of a twig, as Jessie Coon James had gone off with the others. He ate and ate and ate, and when he was done he said, "May I call you Thoreau?"

"That will do nicely," I said. Then I paused — just to let him know that I knew a little bit about him too. I smiled and said, "I will call you Bando."

His eyebrows went up; he cocked his head, shrugged his shoulders, and answered, "That's close enough."

With this, he sat and thought. I felt I had offended him, so I spoke. "I will be glad to help. I will teach you how to live off the land. It is very easy. No one need find you."

His eyebrows gathered together again. This was characteristic of Bando when he was concerned, and so I was sorry I had mentioned his past. After all, outlaw or no outlaw, he was an adult, and I still felt unsure of myself around adults. I changed the subject.

"Let's get some sleep," I said.

"Where do you sleep?" he asked. All this

time sitting and talking with me, and he had not seen the entrance to my tree. I was pleased. Then I beckoned, walked a few feet to the left, pushed back the deer-hide door, and showed Bando my secret.

"Thoreau," he said, "you are quite wonderful." He went in. I lit the turtle candle for him. He explored, tried the bed, came out, and shook his head until I thought it would roll off.

We didn't say much more that night. I let him sleep on my bed. His feet hung off, but he was comfortable, he said. I stretched out by the fire. The ground was dry, the night warm, and I could sleep on anything now.

I got up early and had breakfast ready when Bando came stumbling out of the tree. We ate crayfish, and he really honestly seemed to like them. It takes a little time to acquire a taste for wild foods, so Bando surprised me the way he liked the menu. Of course he was hungry, and that helped.

That day we didn't talk much, just went over the mountain collecting foods. I wanted to dig up the tubers of the Solomon's-seal from a big garden of them on the other side of the gorge. We fished, we swam a little, and I told him I hoped to make a raft pretty soon, so I could float into deeper water and perhaps catch bigger fish.

When Bando heard this, he took my ax and immediately began to cut young trees for this purpose. I watched him and said, "You must have lived on a farm or something."

At that moment a bird sang.

"The wood peewee," said Bando, stopping his work. He stepped into the woods, seeking it. Now I was astonished.

"How would you know about a wood peewee in your business?" I grew bold enough to ask.

"And just what do you think my business is?" he said as I followed him.

"Well, you're not a minister."

"Right!"

"And you're not a doctor or a lawyer."

"Correct."

"You're not a businessman or a sailor."

"No, I am not."

"Nor do you dig ditches."

"I do not."

"Well . . ."

"Guess."

Suddenly I wanted to know for sure. So I said it.

"You are a murderer or a thief or a racketeer, and you are hiding out."

Bando stopped looking for the peewee. He turned and stared at me. At first I was frightened. A bandit might do anything. But he wasn't mad; he was laughing. He had a good deep laugh, and it kept coming out of him. I smiled, then grinned and laughed with him.

"What's funny, Bando?" I asked.

"I like that," he finally said. "I like that a lot." The tickle deep inside him kept him chuckling. I had no more to say, so I ground my heel in the dirt while I waited for him to get over the fun and explain it all to me.

"Thoreau, my friend, I am just a college English teacher lost in the Catskills. I came out to hike around the woods, got completely lost yesterday, found your fire, and fell asleep beside it. I was hoping the Scoutmaster and his troop would be back for supper and help me home."

"Oh no." My comment. Then I laughed. "You see, Bando, before I found you I heard squad cars screaming up the road. Occasionally you read about bandits that hide out in the forest, and I was just so sure that you were someone they were looking for."

ve up the peewee and went back to

the raft making, talking very fast now and laughing a lot. He was fun. Then something sad occurred to me.

"Well, if you're not a bandit, you will have to go home very soon, and there is no point in teaching you how to live on fish and bark and plants."

"I can stay a little while," he said. "This is summer vacation. I must admit I had not planned to eat crayfish on my vacation, but I am rather getting to like it.

"Maybe I can stay until your school opens," he went on. "That's after Labor Day, isn't it?"

I was very still, thinking how to answer that.

Bando sensed this. Then he turned to me with a big grin.

"You really mean you are going to try to winter it out here?"

"I think I can."

"Well!" He sat down, rubbed his forehead in his hands, and looked at me. "Thoreau, I have led a varied life — dishwasher, sax player, teacher. To me it has been an interesting life. Just now it seems very dull." He sat awhile with his head down, then looked up at the mountains and the rocks and trees. I heard him sigh.

"Let's go fish. We can finish this another day."

That is how I came to know Bando. We became very good friends in the week or ten days that he stayed with me, and he helped me a lot. We spent several days gathering white oak acorns and groundnuts, harvesting the blueberry crop and smoking fish.

We flew Frightful every day just for the pleasure of lying on our backs in the meadow and watching her mastery of the sky. I had lots of meat, so what she caught those days was all hers. It was a pleasant time — warm, with occasional thunder showers, some of which we stayed out in. We talked about books. He did know a lot of books, and could quote exciting things from them.

One day Bando went to town and came back with five pounds of sugar.

"I want to make blueberry jam," he announced. "All those excellent berries and no jam."

He worked two days at this. He knew how to make jam. He'd watched his pa make it in Mississippi, but we got stuck on what to put

this one night:

"August 29

"The raft is almost done. Bando has promised to stay until we can sail out into the deep fishing holes.

"Bando and I found some clay along the stream bank. It was as slick as ice. Bando thought it would make good pottery. He shaped some jars and lids. They look good — not Wedgwood, he said, but containers. We dried them on the rock in the meadow, and later Bando made a clay oven and baked them in it. He thinks they might hold the blueberry jam he has been making.

"Bando got the fire hot by blowing on it with some homemade bellows that he fashioned from one of my skins that he tied together like a balloon. A reed is the nozzle.

"August 30

"It was a terribly hot day for Bando to be firing clay jars, but he stuck with it. They look jamworthy, as he says, and he filled three of them tonight. The jam is good, the pots remind me of crude flower pots without the hole in the bottom. Some of the lids don't fit. Bando says he will go home and read more about pottery making so that he can do a better job next time.

"We like the jam. We eat it on hard acorn pancakes.

"Later. Bando met The Baron Weasel today for the first time. I don't know where The Baron has been this past week, but sud-

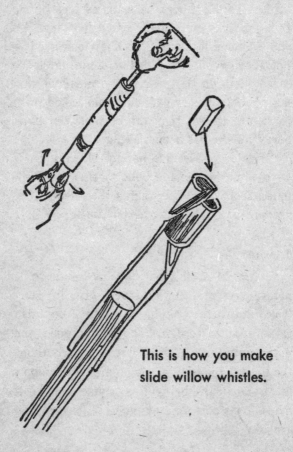

This is how you make slide willow whistles.

denly he appeared on the rock and nearly jumped down Bando's shirt collar. Bando said he liked The Baron best when he was in his hole.

"September 3

"Bando taught me how to make willow whistles today. He and I went to the stream and cut two whistles about eight inches long. He slipped the bark on them. That means he pulled the wood out of the bark, leaving a tube. He made a mouthpiece at one end, cut a hole beneath it, and used the wood to slide up and down like a trombone.

"We played music until the moon came up. Bando could even play jazz on the willow whistles. They are wonderful instruments, sounding much like the wind in the top of the hemlocks. Sad tunes are best suited to willow whistles. When we played 'The Young Voyageur' tears came to our eyes, it was so sad."

There were no more notes for many days. Bando had left me saying, "Good-bye, I'll see you at Christmas." I was so lonely that I kept sewing on my moccasins to keep myself busy. I sewed every free minute for four days, and when they were finished I began a glove to protect my hand from Frightful's sharp talons.

One day when I was thinking very hard about being alone, Frightful gave her gentle call of love and contentment. I looked up.

"Bird," I said, "I had almost forgotten how we used to talk." She made tiny movements with her beak and fluffed her feathers. This was a language I had forgotten since Bando came. It meant she was glad to see me and hear me, that she was well fed and content. I picked her up and squeaked into her neck feathers. She moved her beak, turned her bright head, and bit my nose very gently.

Jessie Coon James came down from the trees for the first time in ten days. He finished my fish dinner. Then, just before dusk, The Baron came up on his boulder and scratched and cleaned and played with a fern leaf.

I had the feeling we were all back together again.

In Which the Autumn
Provides Food and Loneliness

SEPTEMBER BLAZED A TRAIL into the mountains. First she burned the grasses. The grasses seeded and were harvested by the mice and the winds.

Then she sent the squirrels and chipmunks running boldly through the forest, collecting and hiding nuts.

Then she frosted the aspen leaves and left them sunshine yellow.

Then she gathered the birds together in flocks, and the mountaintop was full of songs and twitterings and flashing wings. The birds were ready to move to the south.

And I, Sam Gribley, felt just wonderful, just wonderful.

I pushed the raft down the stream and gathered arrowleaf bulbs, cattail tubers, bulrush roots, and the nutlike tubers of the sedges.

And then the crop of crickets appeared, and Frightful hopped all over the meadow snagging them in her great talons and eating them. I tried them, because I had heard they are good. I think it was another species of cricket that was meant. I think the field cricket would taste excellent if you were starving. I was not starving, so I preferred to listen to them. I abandoned the crickets and went back to the goodness of the earth.

I smoked fish and rabbit, dug wild onions by the pouchful, and raced September for her crop.

"October 15

"Today The Baron Weasel looked moldy. I couldn't get near enough to see what was the matter with him, but it occurs to me that he might be changing his summer fur for his white winter mantle. If he is, it is an itchy process. He scratches a lot."

Seeing The Baron changing his mantle for winter awoke the first fears in me. I wrote that note on a little birch bark, curled up on my bed, and shivered.

"The snow and the cold and the long lifeless

104

months are ahead," I thought. The wind was blowing hard and cool across the mountain. I lit my candle, took out the rabbit and squirrel hides I had been saving, and began rubbing and kneading them to softness.

The Baron was getting a new suit for winter. I must have one too. Some fur underwear, some mittens, fur-lined socks.

Frightful, who was sitting on the footpost of the bed, yawned, fluffed, and thrust her head into the slate-gray feathers of her back. She slept. I worked for several hours.

I must say here that I was beginning to wonder if I should not go home for the winter and come back again in the spring. Everything in the forest was getting prepared for the harsh months. Jessie Coon James was as fat as a barrel. He came down the tree slowly, his fat falling in a roll over his shoulders. The squirrels were working and storing food. They were building leaf nests. The skunks had burrows and plugged themselves in at dawn with bunches of leaves. No drafts could reach them.

As I thought of the skunks and all the animals preparing themselves against the winter, I realized suddenly that my tree would be as cold as the air if I did not somehow find a way to heat it.

"NOTES:

"Today I rafted out into the deep pools of the creek to fish. It was a lazy sort of autumn day, the sky clear, the leaves beginning to brighten, the air warm. I stretched out on my back because the fish weren't biting, and hummed.

"My line jerked and I sat up to pull, but was too late. However, I was not too late to notice that I had drifted into the bank — the very bank where Bando had dug the clay for the jam pots.

"At that moment I knew what I was going to do. I was going to build a fireplace of clay, even fashion a little chimney of clay. It would be small, but enough to warm the tree during the long winter.

"Next day

"I dragged the clay up the mountain to my tree in my second best pair of city pants. I tied the bottoms of the legs, stuffed them full, and as I looked down on my strange cargo I thought of scarecrows and Halloween. I thought of the gang dumping ash cans on Third Avenue and soaping up the windows. Suddenly I was terribly lonely. The air smelled of leaves, and the cool wind from the stream hugged me. The warblers in the trees above me seemed gay and glad about their trip south. I stopped halfway up the mountain and dropped my head. I was lonely and on the verge of tears. Suddenly there was a flash, a pricking sensation on my leg, and I looked down in time to see The Baron leap from my pants to the cover of fern.

"He scared the loneliness right out of me. I ran after him and chased him up the mountain, losing him from time to time in the ferns and crowfeet. We stormed into camp an awful sight. The Baron bouncing and screaming ahead of me, and dragging that half scarecrow of clay.

"Frightful took one look and flew to the end of her leash. She doesn't like The Baron, and watches him — well, like a hawk. I don't like to leave her alone. End notes. Must make fireplace."

It took three days to get the fireplace worked out so that it didn't smoke me out of the tree like a bee. It was an enormous problem. In the first place, the chimney sagged because the clay was too heavy to hold itself up, so I had to get some dry grasses to work into it so it could hold its own weight.

I whittled out one of the old knotholes to

let the smoke out, and built the chimney down from this. Of course when the clay dried, it pulled away from the tree, and all the smoke poured back in on me.

So I tried sealing the leak with pine pitch, and that worked all right, but then the funnel over the firebed cracked, and I had to put wooden props under that.

The wooden props burned, and I could see that this wasn't going to work either; so I went down the mountain to the site of the old Gribley farmhouse and looked around for some iron spikes or some sort of metal.

I took the wooden shovel that I had carved from the board and dug around what I thought must have been the back door or possibly the wood house.

I found a hinge, old handmade nails that would come in handy, and finally, treasure of treasures, the axle of an old wagon. It was much too big. I had no hacksaw to cut it into smaller pieces, and I was not strong enough to heat it and hammer it apart. Besides, I didn't have anything but a small wooden mallet I had made.

I carried my trophies home and sat down before my tree to fix dinner and feed Frightful. The evening was cooling down for a frost. I looked at Frightful's warm feathers. I didn't even have a deer hide for a blanket. I had used the two I had for a door and a pair of pants. I wished that I might grow feathers.

I tossed Frightful off my fist, and she flashed through the trees and out over the meadow. She went with a determination strange to her. "She is going to leave," I cried. "I have never seen her fly so wildly." I pushed the smoked fish aside and ran to the meadow. I whistled and whistled and whistled until my mouth was dry and no more whistle came.

I ran onto the big boulder. I could not see her. Wildly I waved the lure. I licked my lips and whistled again. The sun was a cold, steely color as it dipped below the mountain. The air was now brisk, and Frightful was gone. I was sure that she had suddenly taken off on the migration; my heart was sore and pounding. I had enough food, I was sure. Frightful was not absolutely necessary for my survival, but I was now so fond of her. She was more than a bird. I knew I must have her back to talk to and play with if I was going to make it through the winter.

I whistled. Then I heard a cry in the grasses up near the white birches.

In the gathering darkness I saw movement; I think I flew to the spot. And there she was; she had caught herself a bird. I rolled into the grass beside her and clutched her jesses. She didn't intend to leave, but I was going to make sure that she didn't. I grabbed so swiftly that my hand hit a rock and I bruised my knuckles.

The rock was flat and narrow and long; it was the answer to my fireplace. I picked up Frightful in one hand and the stone in the other; and I laughed at the cold, steely sun as it slipped out of sight, because I knew I was going to be warm. This flat stone was what I needed to hold up the funnel and finish my fireplace.

And that's what I did with it. I broke it into two pieces, set one on each side under the funnel, lit the fire, closed the flap of the door, and listened to the wind bring the first frost to the mountain. I was warm.

Then I noticed something dreadful. Frightful was sitting on the bedpost, her head under her wings. She was toppling. She jerked her head out of her feathers. Her eyes looked glassy. "She is sick," I said. I picked her up and stroked her, and we both might have died there if I had not opened the tent flap to get her some water. The cold night air revived her. "Air," I said. "The fireplace used up all the oxygen. I've got to ventilate this place."

We sat out in the cold for a long time, because I was more than a little afraid of what our end might have been.

I put out the fire, took the door down, and wrapped up in it. Frightful and I slept with the good frost nipping our faces.

"NOTES:

"I cut out several more knotholes to let air in and out of the tree room. I tried it today. I have Frightful on my fist, watching her. It's been about two hours, and she hasn't fainted and I haven't gone numb. I can still write and see clearly.

"Test: Frightful's healthy face."

In Which We All Learn
About Halloween

"*October 28*

"I have been up and down the mountain every day for a week, watching to see if walnuts and hickory nuts are ripe. Today I found the squirrels all over the trees, harvesting them furiously, and so I have decided that ripe or not, I must gather them. It's me or the squirrels.

"I tethered Frightful in the hickory tree while I went to the walnut tree and filled pouches. Frightful protected the hickory nuts. She keeps the squirrels so busy scolding her that they don't have time to take the nuts. They are quite terrified by her. It is a good scheme. I shout and bang the tree and keep them away while I gather.

"I have never seen so many squirrels. They hang from the slender branches, they bounce through the limbs, they seem to come from the whole forest. They must pass messages along to each other — messages that tell what kind of nuts and where the trees are."

A few days later, my storehouse rolling with nuts, I began the race for apples. Entering this race were squirrels, raccoons, and a fat old skunk who looked as if he could eat not another bite. He was ready to sleep his autumn meal off, and I resented him because he did not need my apples. However, I did not toy with him.

I gathered what apples I could, cut some in slices, and dried them on the boulder in the sun. Some I put in the storeroom tree to eat right away. They were a little wormy, but it was wonderful to eat an apple again.

Then one night this was all done, the crop was gathered. I sat down to make a few notes when The Baron came sprinting into sight.

He actually bounced up and licked the edges of my turtle-shell bowl, stormed Frightful, and came to my feet.

"Baron Weasel," I said, "it is nearing Halloween. Are you playing tricks or treats?" I handed him the remains of my turtle-soup dinner and, fascinated, watched him devour it.

"NOTE:

"The Baron chews with his back molars, and chews with a ferocity I have not seen in him before. His eyes gleam, the lips curl back from his white pointed teeth, and he frowns like an angry man. If I move toward him, a rumble starts in his chest that keeps me back. He flashes glances at me. It is indeed strange to be looked in the eye by this fearless wild animal. There is something human about his beady glance. Perhaps because that glance tells me something. It tells me he knows who I am and that he does not want me to come any closer."

The Baron Weasel departed after his feast. Frightful, who was drawn up as skinny as a stick, relaxed and fluffed her feathers, and then I said to her, "See, he got his treats. No tricks." Then something occurred to me. I reached inside the door and pulled out my calendar stick. I counted 28, 29, 30, 31.

"Frightful, that old weasel knows. It is Halloween. Let's have a Halloween party."

Swiftly I made piles of cracked nuts,

smoked rabbit, and crayfish. I even added two of my apples. This food was an invitation to the squirrels, foxes, raccoons, opossums, even the birds that lived around me to come have a party.

When Frightful is tethered to her stump, some of the animals and birds will only come close enough to scream at her. So bird and I went inside the tree, propped open the flap, and waited.

Not much happened that night. I learned that it takes a little time for the woodland messages to get around. But they do. Before the party I had been very careful about leaving food out because I needed every mouthful. I took the precaution of rolling a stone in front of my store tree. The harvest moon rose; Frightful and I went to sleep.

At dawn, we abandoned the party. I left the treats out, however. Since it was a snappy gold-colored day, we went off to get some more rabbit skins to finish my winter underwear.

We had lunch along the creek — stewed mussels and wild potatoes. We didn't get back until dusk because I discovered some wild rice in an oxbow of the stream. There was no more than a handful.

Home that night, everything seemed peaceful enough. A few nuts were gone — to the squirrels, I thought. I baked a fish in leaves and ate a small, precious amount of wild rice. It was marvelous! As I settled down to scrape the rabbit skins of the day, my neighbor the skunk marched right into the camp ground and set to work on the smoked rabbit. I made some Halloween notes:

"The moon is coming up behind the aspens. It is as big as a pumpkin and as orange. The winds are cool, the stars are like electric light bulbs. I am just inside the doorway, with my turtle-shell lamp burning so that I can see to write this.

"Something is moving beyond the second hemlock. Frightful is very alert, as if there are things all around us. Halloween was over at midnight last night, but for us it is just beginning. That's how I feel anyhow, but it just may be my imagination.

"I wish Frightful would stop pulling her feathers in and drawing herself up like a spring. I keep thinking that she feels things.

"Here comes Jessie C. James. He will want the venison.

"He didn't get the venison. There was a snarl, and a big raccoon I've never seen walked past him, growling and looking fero-

cious. Jessie C. stood motionless—I might
say, scared stiff. He held his head at an angle
and let the big fellow eat. If Jessie so much
as rolled his eyes, that old coon would sputter
at him."

It grew dark, and I couldn't see much. An
eerie yelp behind the boulder announced that
the red fox of the meadow was nearing. He
gave me goose bumps. He stayed just beyond
my store tree, weaving back and forth on
silent feet. Every now and then he would
cry — a wavery owl-like cry. I wrote some
more:

"The light from my turtle lamp casts leap-
ing shadows. To the beechnuts has come a
small gray animal. I can't make out what —
now I see it. It's a flying squirrel. That sur-
prises me. I've never seen a flying squirrel
around here, but of course I haven't been up
much after sunset."

When it grew too dark to see, I lit a fire,
hoping it would not end the party. It did not,
and the more I watched, the more I realized
that all these animals were familiar with my
camp. A white-footed mouse walked over my
woodpile as if it were his.

I put out the candle and fell asleep when the fire turned to coals. Much later I was awakened by screaming. I lifted my head and looked into the moonlit forest. A few guests, still lingering at the party saw me move and dashed bashfully into the ground cover. One was big and slender. I thought perhaps a mink. As I slowly came awake, I realized that screaming was coming from behind me. Something was in my house. I jumped up and shouted, and two raccoons skittered under my feet. I reached for my candle, slipped on hundreds of nuts, and fell. When I finally got a light and looked about me, I was dismayed to see what a mess my guests had made of my tree house. They had found the cache of acorns and beechnuts and had tossed them all over my bed and floor. The party was getting rough.

I chased the raccoons into the night and stumbled over a third animal, and was struck by a wet stinging spray. It was skunk! I was drenched. As I got used to the indignity and the smell, I saw the raccoons cavort around my fireplace and dodge past me. They were back in my tree before I could stop them.

A bat winged in from the darkness and circled the tallow candle. It was Halloween, and the goblins were at work. I thought of all the ash cans I had knocked over on the streets of New York. It seemed utterly humorless.

Having invited all these neighbors, I was now faced with the problem of getting rid of them. The raccoons were feeling so much at home that they snatched up beechnuts, bits of dried fish and venison, and tossed them playfully into the air. They were too full to eat any more, but were having a marvelous time making toys out of my hard-won winter food supply.

I herded the raccoons out of the tree and laced the door. I was breathing "relief" when I turned my head to the left, for I sensed someone watching me. There in the moonlight, his big ears erect on his head, sat the red fox. He was smiling — I know he was. I shouted, "Stop laughing!" and he vanished like a magician's handkerchief.

All this had awakened Frightful, who was flopping in the dark in the tree. I reached in around the deer flap to stroke her back to calmness. She grabbed me so hard I yelled, and the visitors moved to the edge of my camp at my cry.

Smelling to the sky, bleeding in the hand, and robbed of part of my hard-won food, I threw wood on the fire and sent an enormous shaft of light into the night. Then I shouted. The skunk moved farther away. The raccoons galloped off a few feet and galloped back. I snarled at them. They went to the edge of the darkness and stared at me. I had learned something that night from that very raccoon bossing Jessie C. James: to animals, might is right. I was biggest and I was oldest, and I was going to tell them so. I growled and snarled and hissed and snorted. It worked. They understood and moved away. Some looked back and their eyes glowed. The red eyes chilled me. Never had there been a more real Halloween night. I looked up, expecting to see a witch. The last bat of the season darted in the moonlight. I dove on my bed and tied the door. There are no more notes about Halloween.

In Which I Find Out
What to Do with Hunters

THAT PARTY had a moral ending: don't
feed wild animals! I picked up and counted
my walnuts and hickory nuts. I was glad to
discover there was more mess than loss. I
decided that I would not only live until
spring, but that I still had more nuts than all
the squirrels on Gribley's (including flying
squirrels).

In early November I was awakened one
morning by a shot from a rifle. The hunting
season had begun! I had forgotten all about
that. To hide from a swarm of hunters was
truly going to be a trick. They would be
behind every tree and on every hill and dale.

They would be shooting at everything that moved, and here was I in deerskin pants and dirty brown sweater, looking like a deer.

I decided, like the animals, to stay holed up the first day of the season. I whittled a fork and finished my rabbit-skin underwear. I cracked a lot of walnuts.

The second day of the hunting season I stuck my head out of my door and decided my yard was messy. I picked it up so that it looked like a forest floor.

The third day of the hunting season some men came in and camped by the gorge. I tried to steal down the other side of the mountain to the north stream, found another camp of hunters there, and went back to my tree.

By the end of the week both Frightful and I were in need of exercise. Gun shots were still snapping around the mountain. I decided to go see Miss Turner at the library. About an hour later I wrote this:

"I got as far as the edge of the hemlock grove when a shot went off practically at my elbow. I didn't have Frightful's jesses in my hand, and she took off at the blast. I climbed a tree. There was a hunter so close to me he could have bitten me, but apparently he was busy watching his deer. I was able to get up into the high branches without being seen. First, I looked around for Frightful. I could see her nowhere. I wanted to whistle for her but didn't think I should. I sat still and looked, and wondered if she'd go home.

"I watched the hunter track his deer. The deer was still running. From where I was I could see it plainly, going toward the old Gribley farm site. Quietly I climbed higher and watched. Then of all things, it jumped the stone fence and fell dead.

"I thought I would stay in the tree until the hunter quartered his kill and dragged it out to the road. Ah, then, it occurred to me that he wasn't even going to find that deer. He was going off at an angle, and from what I could see, the deer had dropped in a big bank of dry ferns and would be hard to find.

"It got to be nerve-racking at this point. I could see my new jacket lying in the ferns, and the hunter looking for it. I closed my eyes and mentally steered him to the left.

"Then, good old Frightful! She had winged down the mountain and was sitting in a sapling maple away from the deer. She saw the man and screamed. He looked in her direction; heaven knows what he thought she was, but he turned and started toward her. She rustled her wings, climbed into the sky, and disappeared over my head. I did want to whistle to her, but feared for my deer, myself, and her.

"I hung in the tree and waited about a half an hour. Finally the man gave up his hunt. His friends called, and he went on down the mountain. I went down the tree.

"In the dry ferns lay a nice young buck. I covered it carefully with some of the stones from the fence and more ferns, and rushed home. I whistled, and down from the top of my own hemlock came Frightful. I got a piece of birch bark to write all this on, so I wouldn't get too anxious and go for the deer too soon.

"We will wait until dark to go get our dinner and my new jacket. I am beginning to think I'll have all the deer hide and venison I can use. There must be other lost game on this mountain."

I got the deer after dark, and I was quite right. Before the season was over I got two more deer in the same way. However, with the first deer to work on, the rest of the season passed quickly. I had lots of scraping and preparing to do. My complaint was that I did not dare light a fire and cook that wonderful meat. I was afraid of being spotted.

I ate smoked venison, nut meats, and hawthorn berries. Hawthorn berries taste a little bit like apples. They are smaller and drier than apples. They also have big seeds in them. The hawthorn bush is easy to tell because it has big red shiny thorns on it.

Each day the shooting lessened as the hunters left the hills and went home. As they cleared out, Frightful and I were freer and freer to roam.

The air temperature now was cold enough to preserve the venison, so I didn't smoke the last two deer; and about two weeks after I heard that first alarming shot, I cut off a beautiful steak, built a bright fire, and when the embers were glowing I had myself a real dinner. I soaked some dried puffballs in water, and when they were big and moist I fried them with wild onions and skimpy old wild carrots and stuffed myself until I felt kindly toward all men. I wrote this:

"November 26

"Hunters are excellent friends if used correctly. Don't let them see you, but follow them closely. Preferably use the tops of trees for this purpose, for hunters don't look up. They look down and to the right and left, and straight ahead. So if you stay in the trees, you can not only see what they shoot, but where it falls; and if you are extremely careful, you can sometimes get to it before they do and hide it. That's how I got my third deer."

I had a little more trouble tanning these hides because the water in my oak stump kept freezing at night. It was getting cold. I began wearing my rabbit-fur underwear most of the morning. It was still too warm at noon to keep it on, but it felt good at night. I slept in it until I got my blanket made. I did not scrape the deer hair off my blanket. I liked it on. Because I had grown, one deerskin wouldn't cover me. I sewed part of another one to it.

The third hide I made into a jacket. I just cut a rectangle with a hole in it for my head and sewed on straight wide sleeves. I put enormous pockets all over it, using every scrap I had, including the pouches I had made last summer. It looked like a cross between a Russian military blouse and a carpenter's apron, but it was warm, roomy, and, I thought, handsome.

In Which Trouble Begins

I STOOD IN MY DOORWAY the twenty-third of November dressed from head to toe in deerskins. I was lined with rabbit fur. I had mittens and squirrel-lined moccasins. I was quite excited by my wardrobe.

I whistled, and Frightful came to my fist. She eyed me with her silky black eyes and pecked at my suit.

"Frightful," I said, "this is not food. It is my new suit. Please don't eat it." She peeped softly, fluffed her feathers, and looked gently toward the meadow.

"You are beautiful too, Frightful," I said, and I touched the slate-gray feathers of her

127

back. Very gently I stroked the jet-black ones that came down from her eyes. Those beautiful marks gave her much of her superb dignity. In a sense she had also come into a new suit. Her plumage had changed during the autumn, and she was breathtaking.

We walked to the spring and we looked in. I saw us quite clearly, as there were no longer any frogs to plop in the water and break the mirror with circles and ripples.

"Frightful," I said as I turned and twisted and looked, "we would be quite handsome if it were not for my hair. I need another haircut."

I did the best job I was able to do with a penknife. I made a mental note to make a hat to cover the stray ends.

Then I did something which took me by surprise. I smelled the clean air of November, turned once more to see how the back of my suit looked, and walked down the mountain. I stepped over the stream on the stones. I walked to the road.

Before I could talk myself out of it, I was on my way to town.

As I walked down the road, I kept pretending I was going to the library; but it was Sunday, and I knew the library was closed.

I tethered Frightful just outside town on a stump. I didn't want to attract any attention. Kicking stones as I went and whistling, I walked to the main intersection of town as if I came every Sunday.

I saw the drugstore and began to walk faster, for I was beginning to sense that I was not exactly what everybody saw every day. Eyes were upon me longer than they needed to be.

By the time I got to the drugstore, I was running. I slipped in and went to the magazine stand. I picked up a comic book and began to read.

Footsteps came toward me. Below the bottom pictures I saw a pair of pants and saddle shoes. One shoe went *tap, tap*. The feet did a kind of hop step, and I watched them walk to the other side of me. *Tap, tap, tap* again; a hop step, and the shoes and pants circled me. Then came the voice. "Well, if it isn't Daniel Boone!"

I looked into a face about the age of my own — but a little more puppish, I thought. It had about the same coloring — brown eyes, brown hair — a bigger nose than mine, and more ears, but a very assured face. I said, "Well?" I grinned, because it had been a long time since I had seen a young man my age.

The young man didn't answer; he simply took my sleeve between his fingers and examined it closely. "Did you chew it yourself?" he asked.

I looked at the spot he was examining and said, "Well, no, I pounded it on a rock there, but I did have to chew it a bit around the neck. It stuck me."

We looked at each other then. I wanted to say something, but didn't know where to begin. He picked at my sleeve again.

"My kid brother has one that looks more real than that thing. Whataya got that on for anyway?"

I looked at his clothes. He had on a nice pair of gray slacks, a white shirt opened at the neck, and a leather jacket. As I looked at these things, I found my voice.

"Well, I'd rip anything like you have on all to pieces in about a week."

He didn't answer; he walked around me again.

"Where did you say you came from?"

"I didn't say, but I come from a farm up the way."

"Whatja say your name was?"

"Well, you called me Daniel Boone."

"Daniel Boone, eh?" He walked around me once more and then peered at me.

"You're from New York. I can tell the accent." He leaned against the cosmetic counter. "Come on now, tell me, is this what the kids are wearing in New York now? Is this gang stuff?"

"I am hardly a member of a gang," I said. "Are you?"

"Out here? Naw, we bowl." The conversation went to bowling for a while; then he looked at his watch.

"I gotta go. You sure are a sight, Boone. Whatja doing anyway, playing cowboys and Indians?"

"Come on up to the Gribley farm and I'll show you what I'm doing. I'm doing research. Who knows when we're all going to be blown to bits and need to know how to smoke venison."

"Gee, you New York guys can sure double-talk. What does that mean, 'burn a block down'?"

"No, it means smoke venison," I said. I took a piece out of my pocket and gave it to him. He smelled it and handed it back.

"Man," he said, "whataya do, eat it?"

"I sure do," I answered.

"I don't know whether to send you home to play with my kid brother or call the cops." He shrugged his shoulders and repeated that he had to go. As he left, he called back, "The Gribley farm?"

"Yes. Come on up if you can find it."

I browsed through the magazines until the clerk got anxious to sell me something, and then I wandered out. Most of the people were in church. I wandered around the town and back to the road.

It was nice to see people again. At the outskirts of town a little boy came bursting out of a house with his shoes off, and his mother came bursting out after him. I caught the little fellow by the arm and I held him until his mother picked him up and took him back. As she went up the steps, she stopped and looked at me. She stepped toward the door, and then walked back a few steps and looked at me again. I began to feel conspicuous and took the road to my mountain.

I passed the little old strawberry lady's house. I almost went in, and then something told me to go home.

I found Frightful, untied her, stroked her creamy breast feathers and spoke to her.

"Frightful, I made a friend today. Do you think that is what I had in mind all the time?" The bird whispered.

I was feeling sad as we kicked up the leaves and started home through the forest. On the other hand, I was glad I had met Mr. Jacket, as I called him.. I never asked his name. I had liked him, although we hadn't even had a fight. All the best friends I had I always fought, then got to like them after the wounds healed.

The afternoon darkened. The nuthatches that had been clinking around the trees were silent. The chickadees had vanished. A single crow called from the edge of the road. There were no insects singing; there were no catbirds, nor orioles, nor vireos, nor robins.

"Frightful," I said, "it is winter. It is winter and I have forgotten to do a terribly important thing: stack up a big woodpile." The stupidity of this sent Mr. Jacket right out of my mind, and I bolted down the valley to my mountain. Frightful flapped to keep her balance. As I crossed the stones to my mountain trail, I said to that bird, "Sometimes I wonder if I will make it to spring."

In Which I Pile Up Wood and Go On with Winter

Now I am almost to that snowstorm. The morning after I had the awful thought about the wood, I got up early. I was glad to hear the nuthatches and chickadees. They gave me the feeling that I still had time to chop. They were bright, busy, and totally unworried about storms. I shouldered my ax and went out.

I had used most of the wood around the hemlock house, so I crossed to the top of the gorge. First I took all the dry limbs off the trees and hauled them home. Then I chopped down dead trees. With wood all around me, I got in my tree and put my arm out. I made an X in the needles. Where the X lay, I began stacking wood. I wanted to be able to reach my wood from the tree when the snow was deep. I piled a big stack at this point. I reached out the other side of the door and made another X. I piled wood here. Then I stepped around my piles and had a fine idea. I decided that if I used up one pile, I could tunnel through the snow to the next and the next. I made many wood piles leading out into the forest.

I watched the sky. It was as blue as summer, but ice was building up along the waterfall at the gorge. I knew winter was coming, although each day the sun would rise in a bright sky and the days would follow cloudless. I piled more wood. This is when I realized that I was scared. I kept cutting wood and piling it like a nervous child biting his nails.

It was almost with relief that I saw the storm arrive.

Now I am back where I began. I won't tell it again; I shall go on now with my relief and the fun and wonderfulness of living on a mountaintop in winter.

The Baron Weasel loved the snow, and was up and about in it every day before Frightful and I had had our breakfast. Professor Bando's jam was my standby on those cold mornings. I would eat mounds of it on my hard acorn pancakes, which I improved by adding hickory nuts. With these as a bracer for the day, Frightful and I would stamp out into the snow and reel down the mountain. She would fly above my head as I slid and plunged and rolled to the creek.

The creek was frozen. I would slide out onto it and break a little hole and ice-fish. The sun would glance off the white snow, the birds would fly through the trees, and I would come home with a fresh meal from the valley. I found there were still plants under the snow, and I would dig down and get teaberry leaves and wintergreen. I got this idea from the deer, who found a lot to eat under the snow. I tried some of the mosses that they liked, but decided moss was for the deer.

Around four o'clock we would all wander home — the nuthatches, the chickadees, the cardinals, Frightful, and I. And now came the nicest part of wonderful days. I would stop in the meadow and throw Frightful off my fist. She would wind into the sky and wait above me as I kicked the grasses. A rabbit would pop up, or sometimes a pheasant. Out of the sky, from a pinpoint of a thing, would dive my beautiful falcon. And, oh, she was beautiful when she made a strike — all power and beauty. On the ground she would cover her quarry. Her perfect feathers would stand up on her body, and her wings would arch over the food. She never touched it until I came and picked her up. I would go home and feed her, then crawl into my tree room, light a little fire on my hearth, and Frightful and I would begin the winter evening.

I had lots of time to cook and try mixing different plants with different meats to make things taste better, and I must say I originated some excellent meals.

When dinner was done, the fire would blaze on; Frightful would sit on the footpost of the bed and preen and wipe her beak and shake. Just the fact that she was alive was a warming thing to know.

I would look at her and wonder what made a bird a bird and a boy a boy. The forest would become silent. I would know The Baron Weasel was about, but I would not hear him.

Then I would get a piece of birch bark and write, or I would make new things out of deer hide, like a hood for Frightful and finally I would take off my suit and my moccasins and crawl into my bed under the sweet-smelling deerskin. The fire would burn itself out and I would be asleep.

Those were nights of the very best sort.

One night I read some of my old notes about how to pile wood so I could get to it under the snow, and I laughed until Frightful awoke. I hadn't made a single tunnel. I walked on the snow to get wood like The Baron Weasel went for food or the deer went for moss.

In Which I Learn About
Birds and People

FRIGHTFUL AND I SETTLED DOWN to living in snow. We went to bed early, slept late, ate the mountain harvest, and explored the country alone. Oh, the deer walked with us, the foxes followed in our footsteps, the winter birds flew over our heads, but mostly we were alone in the white wilderness. It was nice. It was very, very nice. My deerskin rabbit-lined suit was so warm that even when my breath froze in my nostrils, my body was snug and comfortable. Frightful fluffed on the coldest days, but a good flight into the air around the mountain would warm her, and she would come back to my fist with a thump and a flip. This was her signal of good spirits.

I did not become lonely. Many times during the summer I had thought of the "long winter months ahead" with some fear. I had read so much about the loneliness of the farmer, the trapper, the woodsman during the bleakness of winter that I had come to believe it. The winter was as exciting as the summer — maybe more so. The birds were magnificent and almost tame. They talked to each other, warned each other, fought for food, for kingship, and for the right to make the most noise. Sometimes I would sit in my doorway, which became an entrance to behold — a portico of pure white snow, adorned with snowmen — and watch them with endless interest. They reminded me of Third Avenue, and I gave them the names that seemed to fit.

There was Mr. Bracket. He lived on the first floor of our apartment house, and no one could sit on his step or even make a noise near his door without being chased. Mr. Bracket, the chickadee, spent most of his time chasing the young chickadees through the woods. Only his mate could share his favorite perches and feeding places.

Then there were Mrs. O'Brien, Mrs. Calla-

way, and Mrs. Federio. On Third Avenue
they would all go off to the market together
first thing in the morning, talking and pushing and stopping to lecture to children in
gutters and streets. Mrs. Federio always followed Mrs. O'Brien, and Mrs. O'Brien always followed Mrs. Callaway in talking and
pushing and even in buying an apple. And
there they were again in my hemlock —
three busy chickadees. They would flit and
rush around, and click and fly from one eating spot to another. They were noisy, scolding and busily following each other. All the
other chickadees followed them, and they
made way only for Mr. Bracket.

The chickadees, like the people on Third
Avenue, had their favorite routes to and
from the best food supplies. They each had
their own resting perches, and each had a
little shelter in a tree cavity to which they
would fly when the day was over. They would
chatter and call good night and make a big
fuss before they parted; and then the forest
would be as quiet as the apartment house on
Third Avenue when all the kids were off the
streets and all the parents had said their last
words to each other and everyone had gone
to their own little hole.

Sometimes when the wind howled and the

snow blew, the chickadees would be out for only a few hours. Even Mr. Bracket, who had been elected by the chickadees to test whether or not it was too stormy for good hunting, would appear for a few hours and disappear. Sometimes I would find him just sitting quietly on a limb next to the bole of a tree, all fluffed up and doing nothing. There was no one who more enjoyed doing nothing on a bad day than Mr. Bracket of Third Avenue.

Frightful, the two Mr. Brackets, and I shared this feeling. When the ice and sleet and snow drove down through the hemlocks, we all holed up.

I looked at my calendar pole one day and realized that it was almost Christmas. "Bando will come," I thought. "I'll have to prepare a feast and make a present for him. I took stock of the frozen venison and decided that there were enough steaks for us to eat nothing but venison for a month. I scooped under the snow for teaberry plants to boil down and pour over snowballs for dessert.

I checked my cache of wild onions to see if I had enough to make onion soup, and set aside some large, firm groundnuts for mashed potatoes. There were still piles of dogtooth violet bulbs and Solomon's-seal roots and a few dried apples. I cracked walnuts, hickory nuts, and beechnuts; then began a pair of deer-hide moccasins to be lined with rabbit fur for Bando's present. I finished these before Christmas, so I started a hat of the same materials.

Two days before Christmas I began to wonder if Bando would come. He had forgotten, I was sure — or he was busy, I said. Or he thought that I was no longer here and decided not to tramp out through the snows to see. On Christmas Eve Bando still had not arrived, and I began to plan for a very small Christmas with Frightful.

About four thirty Christmas Eve I hung a small red cluster of teaberries on the deerskin door. I went in my tree room for a snack of beechnuts when I heard a faint "halloooo" from far down the mountain. I snuffed out my tallow candle, jumped into my coat and moccasins, and plunged out into the snow. Again a "halloooo" floated over the quiet snow. I took a bearing on the sound and bounced down the hill to meet Bando. I ran into him just as he turned up the valley to follow the stream bed. I was so glad to see him that I hugged him and pounded him on the back.

"Never thought I'd make it," he said. "I

walked all the way from the entrance to the State Park — pretty good, eh?" He smiled and slapped his tired legs. Then he grabbed my arm, and with three quick pinches, tested the meat on me.

"You've been living well," he said. He looked closely at my face. "But you're gonna need a shave in a year or two." I thanked him and we sprang up the mountain, cut across through the gorge and home.

"How's the Frightful?" he asked as soon as we were inside and the light was lit.

I whistled. She jumped to my fist. He got bold and stroked her. "And the jam?" he asked.

"Excellent, except the crocks are absorbent and are sopping up all the juice."

"Well, I brought you some more sugar; we'll try next year. Merry Christmas, Thoreau!" he shouted, and looked about the room.

"I see you have been busy. A blanket, new clothes, and an ingenious fireplace — with a real chimney — and say, you have silverware!" He picked up the forks I had carved.

We ate smoked fish for dinner with boiled dogtooth violet bulbs. Walnuts dipped in jam were dessert. Bando was pleased with his jam.

When we were done, Bando stretched out

on my bed. He propped his feet up and lit his pipe.

"And now, I have something to show you," he said. He reached in his coat pocket and took out a newspaper clipping. It was from a New York paper, and it read:

"WILD BOY SUSPECTED LIVING OFF DEER
AND NUTS IN WILDERNESS OF CATSKILLS"

I looked at Bando and leaned over to read the headline myself.

"Have you been talking?" I asked.

"Me? Don't be ridiculous. You have had several visitors other than me."

"The fire warden — the old lady!" I cried out.

"Now, Thoreau, this could only be a rumor. Just because it is in print doesn't mean it's true. Before you get excited, sit still and listen." He read:

" 'Residents of Delhi, in the Catskill Mountains, report that a wild boy, who lives off deer and nuts, is hiding out in the mountains.

" 'Several hunters stated that this boy stole deer from them during hunting season.' "

"I did not!" I shouted. "I only took the ones they had wounded and couldn't find."

"Well, that's what they told their wives when they came home without their deer. Anyway, listen to this:

"'This wild boy has been seen from time to time by Catskill residents, some of whom believe he is crazy!'"

"Well, that's a terrible thing to say!"

"Just awful," he stated. "Any normal red-blooded American boy wants to live in a tree house and trap his own food. They just don't do it, that's all."

"Read on," I said.

"'Officials say that there is no evidence of any boy living alone in the mountains, and add that all abandoned houses and sheds are routinely checked for just such events. Nevertheless, the residents are sure that such a boy exists!' End story."

"That's a lot of nonsense!" I leaned back against the bedstead and smiled.

"Ho, ho, don't think that ends it," Bando said, and reached in his pocket for another clipping. "This one is dated December fifth, the other was November twenty-third. Shall I read?"

"Yes."

"'OLD WOMAN REPORTS MEETING WILD BOY
WHILE PICKING STRAWBERRIES
IN CATSKILLS

" 'Mrs. Thomas Fielder, ninety-seven, resident of Delhi, N. Y., told this reporter that she met a wild boy on Bitter Mountain last June while gathering her annual strawberry-jelly supply.

" 'She said the boy was brown-haired, dusty, and wandering aimlessly around the mountains. However, she added, he seemed to be in good flesh and happy.

" 'The old woman, a resident of the mountain resort town for ninety-seven years, called this office to report her observation. Local residents report that Mrs. Fielder is a fine old member of the community, who only occasionally sees imaginary things.' "

Bando roared. I must say I was sweating, for I really did not expect this turn of events.

"And now," went on Bando, "and now the queen of the New York papers. This story was buried on page nineteen. No sensationalism for this paper:

" 'BOY REPORTED LIVING OFF LAND
IN CATSKILLS
" 'A young boy of seventeen or eighteen, who left home with a group of Boy Scouts, is reported to be still scouting in that area, according to the fire warden of the Catskill Mountains.

" 'Evidence of someone living in the forest — a fireplace, soup bones, and cracked nuts — was reported by Warden Jim Handy, who spent the night in the wilderness looking for the lad. Jim stated that the young man had apparently left the area, as there was no evidence of his camp upon a second trip —' "

"What second trip?" I asked.

Bando puffed his pipe, looked at me wistfully and said, "Are you ready to listen?"

"Sure," I answered.

"Well, here's the rest of it: '. . . there was no trace of his camp on a second trip, and the warden believes that the young man returned to his home at the end of the summer.'

"You know, Thoreau, I could scarcely drag myself away from the newspapers to come up here. You make a marvelous story."

I said, "Put more wood on the fire, it is Christmas. No one will be searching these mountains until May Day."

Bando asked for the willow whistles. I got them for him, and after running the scale several times he said, "Let us serenade the ingenuity of the American newspaperman. Then let us serenade the conservationists who have protected the American wilderness, so that a boy can still be alone in this world of millions of people."

I thought that was suitable, and we played "Holy Night." We tried "The Twelve Days of Christmas," but the whistles were too stiff and Bando was too tired.

"Thoreau, my body needs rest. Let's give up," he said after two bad starts. I banked the fire and blew out the candle and slept in my clothes.

It was Christmas when we awoke. Breakfast was light — acorn pancakes, jam, and sassafras tea. Bando went for a walk; I lit the fire in the fireplace and spent the morning creating a feast from the wilderness.

I gave Bando his presents when he returned. He liked them. He was really pleased; I could tell by his eyebrows. They went up and down and in and out. Furthermore, I know he liked the presents because he wore them.

The onion soup was about to be served when I heard a voice shouting in the distance, "I know you are there! I know you are there! Where are you?"

"Dad!" I screamed, and dove right through the door onto my stomach. I fell down the mountain shouting, "Dad! Dad! Where are you?" I found him resting in a snowdrift,

looking at the cardinal pair that lived near the stream. He was smiling, stretched out on his back, not in exhaustion, but in joy.

"Merry Christmas!" he whooped. I ran toward him. He jumped to his feet, tackled me, thumped my chest, and rubbed snow in my face.

Then he stood up, lifted me from the snow by the pockets on my coat, and held me off the ground so that we were eye to eye. He sure smiled. He threw me down in the snow again and wrestled with me for a few minutes. Our formal greeting done, we strode up the mountain.

"Well, son," he began, "I've been reading about you in the papers and I could no longer resist the temptation to visit you. I still can't believe you did it."

His arm went around me. He looked real good, and I was overjoyed to see him.

"How did you find me?" I asked eagerly.

"I went to Mrs. Fielder, and she told me which mountain. At the stream I found your raft and ice-fishing holes. Then I looked for trails and footsteps. When I thought I was getting warm, I hollered."

"Am I that easy to find?"

"You didn't have to answer, and I'd probably have frozen in the snow." He was pleased and not angry at me at all. He said again, "I just didn't think you'd do it. I was sure you'd be back the next day. When you weren't, I bet on the next week; then the next month. How's it going?"

"Oh, it's a wonderful life, Dad!"

When we walked into the tree, Bando was putting the final touches on the venison steak.

"Dad, this is my friend, Professor Bando; he's a teacher. He got lost one day last summer and stumbled onto my camp. He liked it so well that he came back for Christmas. Bando, meet my father."

Bando turned the steak on the spit, rose, and shook my father's hand.

"I am pleased to meet the man who sired this boy," he said grandly. I could see that they liked each other and that it was going to be a splendid Christmas. Dad stretched out on the bed and looked around.

"I thought maybe you'd pick a cave," he said. "The papers reported that they were looking for you in old sheds and houses, but I knew better than that. However, I never would have thought of the inside of a tree. What a beauty! Very clever, son; very, very clever. This is a comfortable bed."

He saw my food caches, stood and peered

into them. "Got enough to last until spring?"

"I think so," I said. "If I don't keep getting hungry visitors all the time." I winked at him.

"Well, I would wear out my welcome by a year if I could, but I have to get back to work soon after Christmas."

"How's Mom and all the rest?" I asked as I took down the turtle-shell plates and set them on the floor.

"She's marvelous. How she manages to feed and clothe those eight youngsters on what I bring her, I don't know; but she does it. She sends her love, and says that she hopes you are eating well-balanced meals."

The onion soup was simmering and ready. I gave Dad his.

"First course," I said.

He breathed deeply of the odor and downed it boiling hot.

"Son, this is better onion soup than the chef at the Waldorf can make."

Bando sipped his, and I put mine in the snow to cool.

"Your mother will stop worrying about your diet when she hears of this."

Bando rinsed Dad's soup bowl in the snow, and with great ceremony and elegance — he could really be elegant when the occasion arose — poured him a turtle shell of sassafras tea. Quoting a passage from one of Dickens's food-eating scenes, he carved the blackened steak. It was pink and juicy inside. Cooked to perfection. We were all proud of it. Dad had to finish his tea before he could eat. I was short on bowls. Then I filled his shell. A mound of sort of fluffy mashed cattail tubers, mushrooms, and dogtooth violet bulbs, smothered in gravy thickened with acorn powder. Each plate had a pile of soaked and stewed honey locust beans, mixed with hickory nuts. The beans are so hard it took three days to soak them.

It was a glorious feast. Everyone was impressed, including me. When we were done, Bando went down to the stream and cut some old dried and hollow reeds. He came back and carefully made us each a flute with the tip of his penknife. He said the willow whistles were too old for such an occasion. We all played Christmas carols until dark. Bardo wanted to try some complicated jazz tunes, but the late hour, the small fire dancing and throwing heat, and the snow insulating us from the winds made us all so sleepy that we were not capable of more than a last slow rendition of taps before we put ourselves on and under skins and blew out the light.

Before anyone was awake the next morning, I heard Frightful call hungrily. I had put her outside to sleep, as we were very crowded. I went out to find her. Her Christmas dinner had been a big piece of venison, but the night air had enlarged her appetite. I called her to my fist and we went into the meadow to rustle up breakfast for the guests. She was about to go after a rabbit, but I thought that wasn't proper fare for a post-Christmas breakfast, so we went to the stream. Frightful caught herself a pheasant while I kicked a hole in the ice and did a little ice fishing. I caught about six trout and whistled Frightful to my hand. We returned to the hemlock. Dad and Bando were still asleep, with their feet in each other's faces, but both looking very content.

I built the fire and was cooking the fish and making pancakes when Dad shot out of bed.

"Wild boy!" he shouted. "What a sanguine smell. What a purposeful fire. Breakfast in a tree. Son, I toil from sunup to sundown, and never have I lived so well!"

I served him. He choked a bit on the acorn pancakes — they are a little flat and hard — but Bando got out some of his blueberry jam and smothered the pancakes with an enormous portion. Dad went through the motions of eating this. The fish, however, he enjoyed, and he asked for more. We drank sassafras tea, sweetened with some of the sugar Bando had brought me, rubbed our turtle shells clean in the snow, and went out into the forest.

Dad had not met Frightful. When she winged down out of the hemlock, he ducked and flattened out in the snow shouting, "Blast off!"

He was very cold toward Frightful until he learned that she was the best provider we had ever had in our family, and then he continually praised her beauty and admired her talents. He even tried to pet her, but Frightful was not to be won. She snagged him with her talons.

They stayed away from each other for the rest of Dad's visit, although Dad never ceased to admire her from a safe distance.

Bando had to leave two or three days after Christmas. He had some papers to grade, and he started off reluctantly one morning, looking very unhappy about the way of life he had chosen. He shook hands all around and then turned to me and said, "I'll save all the newspaper clippings for you, and if they start getting too hot on your trail, I'll call the New York papers and give them a bum steer." I could see he rather liked the idea, and departed a little happier.

Dad lingered on for a few more days, ice fishing, setting my traps and snares, and husking walnuts. He whittled some cooking spoons and forks.

On New Year's Day he said he must go.

"I told your mother I would only stay for Christmas. It's a good thing she knows me, or she might be worried."

"She won't send the police out to look for you?" I asked hurriedly. "Could she think you never found me?"

"Oh, I told her I'd call her Christmas night if I didn't." He poked around for another hour or two, trying to decide just how to leave. Finally he started down the mountain. He had hardly gone a hundred feet before he was back.

"I've decided to leave by another route. Somebody might backtrack me and find you. And that would be too bad." He came over to me and put his hand on my shoulder. "You've done very well, Sam." He grinned and walked toward the gorge.

I watched him bound from rock to rock. He waved from the top of a large rock leaped into the air. That was the last I saw of Dad for a long time.

In Which I Have a
Good Look at Winter and Find
Spring in the Snow

WITH CHRISTMAS OVER, the winter became serious. The snows deepened, the wind blew, the temperatures dropped until the air snapped and talked. Never had humanity seemed so far away as it did in those cold still months of January, February, and March. I wandered the snowy crags, listening to the language of the birds by day and to the noises of the weather by night. The wind howled, the snow avalanched, and the air creaked.

I slept, ate, played my reed whistle, and talked to Frightful.

To be relaxed, warm, and part of the winter wilderness is an unforgettable experience. I was in excellent condition. Not a cold, not a sniffle, not a moment of fatigue. I enjoyed the feeling that I could eat, sleep, and be warm, and outwit the storms that blasted the mountains and the subzero temperatures that numbed them.

It snowed on. I plowed through drifts and stamped paths until eventually it occurred to me that I had all the materials to make snowshoes for easier traveling.

Here are the snowshoe notes:

"I made slats out of ash saplings, whittling them thin enough to bow. I soaked them in water to make them bend more easily, looped the two ends together, and wound them with hide.

"With my penknife I made holes an inch apart all around the loop.

"I strung deer hide crisscross through the loops. I made a loop of hide to hold my toe and straps to tie the shoes on.

"When I first walked in these shoes, I tripped on my toes and fell, but by the end of the first day I could walk from the tree to the gorge in half the time."

I lived close to the weather. It is surprising how you watch it when you live in it. Not a cloud passed unnoticed, not a wind blew untested. I knew the moods of the storms, where they came from, their shapes and colors. When the sun shone, I took Frightful to the meadow and we slid down the mountain on my snapping-turtle-shell sled. She really didn't care much for this.

When the winds changed and the air smelled like snow, I would stay in my tree, because I had gotten lost in a blizzard one afternoon and had had to hole up in a rock ledge until I could see where I was going. That day the winds were so strong I could not push against them, so I crawled under the ledge; for hours I wondered if I would be able to dig out when the storm blew on. Fortunately I only had to push through about a foot of snow. However, that taught me to stay home when the air said "snow." Not that I was afraid of being caught far from home in a storm, for I could find food and shelter and make a fire anywhere, but I had become as attached to my hemlock house as a brooding bird to her nest. Caught out in the storms and weather, I had an urgent desire to return to my tree, even as The Baron Weasel returned to his den, and the deer to their copse. We all had our little "patch" in the wilderness. We all fought to return there.

I usually came home at night with the nuthatch that roosted in a nearby sapling. I knew I was late if I tapped the tree and he came out. Sometimes when the weather was icy and miserable, I would hear him high in the trees near the edge of the meadow, yanking and yanking and flicking his tail, and then I would see him wing to bed early. I considered him a pretty good barometer; and if he went to his tree early, I went to mine early too. When you don't have a newspaper or radio to give you weather bulletins, watch the birds and animals. They can tell when a storm is coming. I called the nuthatch "Barometer," and when he holed up I holed up, lit my light, and sat by my fire whittling or learning new tunes on my reed whistle. I was now really into the teeth of winter, and quite fascinated by its activity. There is no such thing as a "still winter night." Not only are many animals running around in the creaking cold, but the trees cry out and limbs snap and fall, and the wind gets caught in a ravine and screams until it dies. One noisy night I put this down:

"There is somebody in my bedroom. I can hear small exchanges of greetings and little

feet moving up the wall. By the time I get to
my light all is quiet.

"Next day

"There was something in my room last
night — a small tunnel leads out from my
door into the snow. It is a marvelous tunnel,
neatly packed, and it goes from a dried fern
to a clump of moss. Then it turns and disap-
pears. I would say, mouse.

"That night

"I kept an ember glowing and got a fast
light before the visitor could get to the door.
It *was* a mouse — a perfect little white-
footed deer mouse with enormous black eyes
and tidy white feet. Caught in the act of in-
truding, he decided not to retreat, but came
toward me a few steps. I handed him a nut
meat. He took it in his fragile paws, stuffed
it in his cheek, flipped, and went out his secret tunnel. No doubt the tunnel leads right
over to my store tree, and this fellow is having a fat winter."

There were no raccoons or skunks about
in the snow, but the mice, the weasels, the
mink, the foxes, the shrews, the cottontail

rabbits were all busier than Coney Island in July. Their tracks were all over the mountain, and their activities ranged from catching each other to hauling various materials back to their burrows for more insulation.

By day the birds were awing. They got up late, after I did, and would call to each other before hunting. I would stir up my fire and think about how much food it must take to keep one little bird alive in that fierce cold. They must eat and eat and eat, I thought.

Once, however, I came upon a male cardinal sitting in a hawthorn bush. It was a miserable day — gray, damp, and somewhere around the zero mark. The cardinal wasn't doing anything at all — just sitting on a twig, all fluffed up to keep himself warm. "Now there's a wise bird," I said to myself. "He is conserving his energy — none of this flying around looking for food and wasting effort." As I watched him, he shifted his feet twice, standing on one and pulling the other up into his warm feathers. I had often wondered why birds' feet didn't freeze, and there was my answer. He even sat down on both of them and let his warm feathers cover them like socks.

"I took Frightful out today. We went over to the meadow to catch a rabbit for her. As we passed one of the hemlocks near the edge of the grove, she pulled her feathers to her body and looked alarmed. I tried to find out what had frightened her, but saw nothing.

"On the way back, we passed the same tree and I noticed an owl pellet cast in the snow. I looked up. There were lots of limbs and darkness, but I could not see the owl. I walked around the tree; Frightful stared at one spot until I thought her head would swivel off. I looked, and there it was, looking like a broken limb: a great horned owl. I must say I was excited to have such a neighbor. I hit the tree with a stick and he flew off. Those great wings — they must have been five feet across — beat the wind, but there was no sound. The owl steered down the mountain through the tree limbs, and somewhere not far away he vanished in the needles and limbs.

"It is really very special to have a horned owl. I guess I feel this way because he is such a wilderness bird. He needs lots of forest and big trees, and so his presence means that the Gribley farm is a beautiful place indeed."

One week the weather gave a little to the sun, and snow melted and limbs dumped their loads and popped up into the air. I thought I'd try to make an igloo. I was cutting big blocks of snow and putting them in a circle. Frightful was dozing with her face in the sun, and the tree sparrows were raiding the hemlock cones. I worked and hummed, and did not notice the gray sheet of cloud that was sneaking up the mountain from the northwest. It covered the sun suddenly. I realized the air was damp enough to wring. I could stay as warm as a bug if I didn't get wet, so I looked at the drab mess in the sky, whistled for Frightful, and started back to the tree. We holed up just as Barometer was yanking his way home and it was none too soon. It drizzled, it misted, it sprinkled, and finally it froze. The deer hide grew stiff with ice as darkness came, and it rattled like a piece of tin when the wind hit it.

I made a fire, the tree room warmed, and I puttered around with a concoction I call possum sop. A meal of frozen possum stewed with lichens, snakeweed, and lousewort. It is a different sort of dish. Of course what I really like about it are the names of all the plants with the name possum. I fooled for an hour or so brewing this dish, adding this and that, when I heard the mouse in his tunnel. I realized he was making an awful fuss, and decided it was because he was trying to gnaw through ice to get in. I decided to help him. Frightful was on her post, and I wanted to see the mouse's face when he found he was in a den with a falcon. I pushed the deerskin door. It wouldn't budge. I kicked it. It gave a little, cracking like china, and I realized that I was going to be iced in if I didn't keep that door open.

I finally got it open. There must have been an inch and a half of ice on it. The mouse, needless to say, was gone. I ate my supper and reminded myself to awaken and open the door off and on during the night. I put more wood on the fire, as it was damp in spite of the flames, and went to bed in my underwear and suit.

I awoke twice and kicked open the door. Then I fell into a sound sleep that lasted hours beyond my usual rising time. I overslept, I discovered, because I was in a block of ice, and none of the morning sounds of the forest penetrated my glass house to awaken me. The first thing I did was try to open the door; I chipped and kicked and managed to get my head out to see what had happened.

I was sealed in. Now, I have seen ice storms, and I know they can be shiny and glassy and treacherous, but this was something else. There were sheets of ice binding the aspens to earth and cementing the tops of the hemlocks in arches. It was inches thick! Frightful winged out of the door and flew to a limb, where she tried to perch. She slipped, dropped to the ground, and skidded on her wings and undercoverts to a low spot where she finally stopped. She tried to get to her feet, slipped, lost her balance, and spread her wings. She finally flapped into the air and hovered there until she could locate a decent perch. She found one close against the bole of the hemlock. It was ice-free.

I laughed at her, and then I came out and took a step. I landed with an explosion on my seat. The jolt splintered the ice and sent glass-covered limbs clattering to earth like a shopful of shattering crystal. As I sat there — and I didn't dare to move because I hurt — I heard an enormous explosion. It was followed by splintering and clattering and smashing. A maple at the edge of the meadow had literally blown up. I feared now for my trees — the ice was too heavy to bear. While down, I chipped the deer flap clean, and sort of swam back into my tree, listening to trees exploding all over the mountain. It was a fearful and dreadful sound. I lit a fire, ate smoked fish and dried apples, and went out again. I must say I toyed with the idea of making ice skates. However, I saw the iron wagon axle iced against a tree, and crawled to it. I de-iced it with the butt of my ax, and used it for a cane. I would stab it into the ground and inch along. I fell a couple of times, but not as hard as that first time.

Frightful saw me start off through the woods, for I had to see this display, and she winged to my shoulder, glad for a good perch. At the meadow I looked hopefully for the sun, but it didn't have a chance. The sky was as thick as Indiana bean soup. Out in the open I watched one tree after another splinter and break under the ice, and the glass sparks that shot into the air and the thunder that the ice made as it shattered were something to remember.

At noon not a drip had fallen; the ice was as tight as it had been at dawn. I heard no nuthatches; the chickadees called once, but were silent again. There was an explosion near my spring. A hemlock had gone. Frightful and I crept back to the tree. I decided that if my house was going to shatter, I would just as soon be in it. Inside, I threw sticks to

Frightful and she caught them in her talons. This is a game we play when we are tense and bored. Night came, and the ice still lay in sheets. We slept to the occasional boom of breaking trees, although the explosions were not as frequent. Apparently the most rotted and oldest trees had collapsed first. The rest were more resilient, and unless a wind came up, I figured the damage was over.

At midnight a wind came up. It awakened me, for the screech of the iced limbs rubbing each other and the snapping of the ice sounded like a madhouse. I listened, decided there was nothing I could do, buried my head under the deer hide, and went back to sleep.

Around six or seven I heard Barometer, the nuthatch. He yanked as he went food hunting through the hemlock grove. I jumped up and looked out. The sun had come through, and the forest sparkled and shone in cruel splendor.

That day I heard the *drip*, *drip* begin, and by evening some of the trees had dumped their loads and were slowly lifting themselves to their feet, so to speak. The aspens and birch trees, however, were still bent like Indian bows.

Three days later the forest arose, the ice

melted, and for about a day or so we had warm, glorious weather.

The mountain was a mess. Broken trees, fallen limbs were everywhere. I felt badly about the ruins until I thought that this had been happening to the mountain for thousands of years and the trees were still there, as were the animals and birds. The birds were starved, and many died. I found their cold little bodies under bushes, and one stiff chickadee in a cavity. Its foot was drawn into its feathers, its feathers were fluffed.

Frightful ate old frozen muskrat during those days. We couldn't kick up a rabbit or even a mouse. They were in the snow under the ice, waiting it out. I suppose the mice went right on tunneling to the grasses and the mosses, and had no trouble staying alive, but I did wonder how the cottontails and The Baron Weasel were doing. I needn't have. Here are some notes about him:

"I should not have worried about The Baron Weasel: he appeared after the ice storm, looking sleek and pleased with himself. I think he dined royally on the many dying animals and birds. In any event, he was full of pep and ran up the hemlock to chase Frightful off her perch. That Baron!

It's a good thing I don't have to tie Frightful much any more, or he would certainly try to kill her. He still attacks me — more for the fun of being sent sprawling out into the snow than for food, for he hasn't put his teeth in my trousers for months."

January was a fierce month. After the ice storm came more snow. The mountaintop was never free of it, the gorge was blocked; only on the warmest days could I hear, deep under the ice, the trickle of water seeping over the falls. I still had food, but it was getting low. All the fresh frozen venison was gone, and most of the bulbs and tubers. I longed for just a simple dandelion green.

Toward the end of January I began to feel tired, and my elbows and knees were a little stiff. This worried me. I figured it was due to some vitamin I wasn't getting, but I couldn't remember which vitamin it was or even where I would find it if I could remember it.

One morning my nose bled. It frightened me a bit, and I wondered if I shouldn't hike to the library and reread the material on vitamins. I was sure that was the trouble. It didn't last long, however, so I figured it wasn't too serious. I decided I would last until the greens came to the land, for I was of the opinion that since I had had nothing green for months, that was the trouble.

On that same day Frightful caught a rabbit in the meadow. As I cleaned it, the liver suddenly looked so tempting that I could hardly wait to prepare it. For the next week, I really craved every liver and took them from her with hunger. The tiredness ended, the bones stopped aching, and I had no more nosebleeds. Hunger is a funny thing. It has a kind of intelligence all its own. I ate liver almost every day until the first plants emerged, and I never had any more trouble. I have looked up vitamins since. I am not surprised to find that liver is rich in vitamin C. So are citrus fruits and green vegetables, the foods I lacked. Wild plants like sorrel and dock are rich in this vitamin too. Even if I had known this then, it would have done me no good, for they were but roots in the earth. As it turned out, liver was the only available source of vitamin C — and on liver I stuffed, without knowing why.

So much for my health. I wonder now why I didn't have more trouble than I did, except that my mother worked in a children's hospital during the war, helping to prepare food, and she was conscious of what made up a balanced meal. We heard a lot about it as kids, so I was not unaware that my winter diet was off balance.

After that experience, however, I noticed things in the forest that I hadn't paid any attention to before. A squirrel had stripped the bark off a sapling at the foot of the meadow, leaving it gleaming white. I pondered when I saw it, wondering if he had lacked a vitamin or two and had sought it in the bark. I must admit I tried a little of the bark myself, but decided that even if it was loaded with vitamins, I preferred liver.

I also noticed that the birds would sit in the sun when it favored our mountain with its light, and I, being awfully vitamin-minded at the time, wondered if they were gathering vitamin D. To be on the safe side, in view of this, I sat in the sun too when it was out. So did Frightful.

My notes piled up during these months, and my journal of birch bark became a storage problem. I finally took it out of my tree and cached it under a rock ledge nearby. The mice made nests in it, but it held up even when it got wet. That's one thing about using the products of the forest: they are usually weatherproof. This is important when the weather is as near to you as your skin and as much a part of your life as eating.

I was writing more about the animals now and less about myself, which proves I was feeling pretty safe. Here is an interesting entry:

"February 6

"The deer have pressed in all around me. They are hungry. Apparently they stamp out yards in the valleys where they feed during the dawn and dusk, but many of them climb back to the hemlock grove to hide and sleep for the day. They manage the deep snows so effortlessly on those slender hooves. If I were to know that a million years from today my children's children's children were to live as I am living in these mountains, I should marry me a wife with slender feet and began immediately to breed a race with hooves, that the Catskill children of the future might run through the snows and meadows and marshes as easily as the deer."

I got to worrying about the deer, and for many days I climbed trees and cut down tender limbs for them. At first only two came, then five, and soon I had a ring of large-eyed, white-tailed deer, waiting at my tree at twilight for me to come out and chop off limbs. I was astonished to see this herd grow, and wondered what signals they used to inform each other of my services. Did they smell fatter? Look more contented? Somehow they were able to tell their friends that there was a free lunch on my side of the mountain, and more and more arrived.

One evening there were so many deer that I decided to chop limbs on the other side of the meadow. They were cutting up the snow and tearing up the ground around my tree with their pawing.

Three nights later they all disappeared. Not one deer came for limbs. I looked down the valley, and in the dim light could see the open earth on the land below. The deer could forage again. Spring was coming to the land! My heart beat faster. I think I was trembling. The valley also blurred. The only thing that can do that is tears, so I guess I was crying.

That night the great horned owls boomed out across the land. My notes read:

"February 10

"I think the great horned owls have eggs! The mountain is white, the wind blows, the snow is hard-packed, but spring is beginning in the hollow in the maple. I will climb it tomorrow.

"Yes, yes, yes, yes, it is spring in the maple. Two great horned-owl eggs lie in the cold snow-rimmed cavity in the broken top of the tree. They were warm to my touch. Eggs in the snow: now isn't that wonderful? I didn't stay long, for it is bitter weather and I wanted the female to return immediately. I climbed down, and as I ran off toward my tree I saw her drift on those muffled wings of the owl through the limbs and branches as she went back to her work. I crawled through the tunnel of ice that leads to my tree now, the wind beating at my back. I spent the evening whittling and thinking about the owl high in the forest with the first new life of the spring."

And so with the disappearance of the deer, the hoot of the owl, the cold land began to create new life. Spring is terribly exciting when you are living right in it.

I was hungry for green vegetables, and that night as I went off to sleep I thought of the pokeweeds, the dandelions, the spring beauties that would soon be pressing up from the earth.

More About the Spring in the Winter and the Beginning of My Story's End

THE OWL had broken the spell of winter. From that time on things began to happen that you'd have to see to believe. Insects appeared while the snow was on the ground. Birds built nests, raccoons mated, foxes called to each other, seeking again their lifelong mates. At the end of February the sap began to run in the maple trees. I tapped some trees and boiled the sap to syrup. It takes an awful lot of sap to make one cup of syrup, I discovered — thirty-two cups, to be exact.

All this and I was still in my winter fur-lined underwear. One or two birds returned, the ferns by the protected spring unrolled

— very slowly, but they did. Then the activity gathered momentum, and before I was aware of the change, there were the skunk cabbages poking their funny blooms above the snow in the marsh. I picked some and cooked them, but they aren't any good. A skunk cabbage is a skunk cabbage.

From my meadow I could see the valleys turning green. My mountain was still snow-capped, so I walked into the valleys almost every day to scout them for edible plants. Frightful rode down with me on my shoulder. She knew even better than I that the season had changed, and she watched the sky like radar. No life traveled that sky world unnoticed by Frightful. I thought she wanted to be free and seek a mate, but I could not let her. I still depended upon her talents and company. Furthermore, she was different, and if I did let her go she probably would have been killed by another female, for Frightful had no territory other than the hemlock patch and her hunting instincts had been trained for man. She was a captive, not a wild, bird, and that is almost another kind of bird.

One day I was in the valley digging tubers and collecting the tiny new dandelion shoots when Frightful saw another duck hawk and flew from my shoulder like a bolt, pulling the leash from my hand as she went.

"Frightful!" I called. "You can't leave me now!" I whistled, held out a piece of meat, and hoped she would not get her leash caught in a treetop. She hovered above my head, looked at the hawk and then at my hand, folded her wings, and dropped to my fist.

"I saw that!" a voice said. I spun around to see a young man about my own age, shivering at the edge of the woods.

"You're the wild boy, aren't you?"

I was so astonished to see a human being in all this cold, thawing silence that I just stood and looked at him. When I gathered my wits I replied, "No, I'm just a citizen."

"Aw, gee," he said with disappointment. Then he gave in to the cold and shivered until the twigs around him rattled. He stepped forward.

"Well, anyway, I'm Matt Spell. I work after school on the Poughkeepsie *New Yorker,* a newspaper. I read all the stories about the wild boy who lives in the Catskills, and I thought that if I found him and got a good story, I might get to be a reporter. Have you ever run across him? Is there such a boy?"

"Aw, it's all nonsense," I said as I gathered some dry wood and piled it near the edge of the woods. I lit it swiftly, hoping he would not notice the flint and steel. He was so cold and so glad to see the flames that he said nothing.

I rolled a log up to the fire for him and shoved it against a tree that was blocked from the raw, biting wind by a stand of hawthorns. He crouched over the flames for a long time, then practically burnt the soles off his shoes warming his feet. He was that miserable.

"Why didn't you dress warmer for this kind of a trip?" I asked. "You'll die up here in this damp cold."

"I think I am dying," he said, sitting so close to the fire, he almost smothered it. He was nice-looking, about thirteen or fourteen, I would have said. He had a good bold face, blue eyes, hair about the color of my stream in the thaw. Although he was big, he looked like the kind of fellow who didn't know his own strength. I liked Matt.

"I've still got a sandwich," he said. "Want half?"

"No, thanks," I said. "I brought my lunch." Frightful had been sitting on my shoulder through all this, but now the smoke was bothering her and she hopped to a higher perch. I still had her on the leash.

"There was a bird on your shoulder," Matt said. "He had nice eyes. Do you know him?"

"I'm sort of an amateur falconer," I replied. "I come up here to train my bird. It's a she — Frightful is her name."

"Does she catch anything?"

"Now and then. How hungry are you?" I asked as his second bite finished the sandwich.

"I'm starved. But don't share your lunch; I have some money. Just tell me which road takes you toward the Hudson River."

I stood up and whistled to Frightful. She flew down. I undid her leash from her jesses. I stroked her head for a moment, then threw her into the air and walked out into the field, kicking the brush as I went.

I had noticed a lot of rabbit tracks earlier, and followed them over the muddy earth as best I could. I kicked up a rabbit, and with a twist Frightful dropped out of the sky and took it.

Roast rabbit is marvelous under any conditions, but when you're cold and hungry it is superb. Matt enjoyed every bite. I worked on a small portion to be sociable, for I was not especially hungry. I dared not offer him the walnuts in my pocket, for too much had been written about that boy living off nuts.

"My whole circulatory system thanks you," Matt said. He meant it, for his hands and feet were now warm, and the blue color had left his lips and was replaced by a good warm red.

"By the way, what's your name?"

"Sam. Sam Gribley," I said.

"Sam, if I could borrow a coat from you, I think I could make it to the bus station without freezing to death. I sure didn't think it would be so much colder in the mountains. I could mail it back to you."

"Well," I hesitated, "my house is pretty far from here. I live on the Gribley farm, and just come down here now and then to hunt with the falcon; but maybe we could find an old horse blanket or something in one of the deserted barns around here."

"Aw, never mind, Sam. I'll run to keep warm. Have you any ideas about this wild boy — seen anyone that you think the stories might be referring to?"

"Let's start toward the road," I said as I stamped out the fire. I wound him through the forest until I was dizzy and he was lost, then headed for the road. At the edge of the woods I said, "Matt, I have seen that boy."

Matt Spell stopped.

"Gee, Sam, tell me about him." I could hear

paper rattle, and saw that Matt's cold hands were not too stiff to write in his notebook.

We walked down the road a bit and then I said, "Well, he ran away from home one day and never went back."

"Where does he live? What does he wear?"

We sat down on a stone along the edge of the road. It was behind a pine tree, and out of the ripping wind.

"He lives west of here in a cave. He wears a bearskin coat, has long hair — all matted and full of burrs — and according to him he fishes for a living."

"You've talked to him?" he asked brightly.

"Oh yes, I talk to him."

"Oh, this is great!" He wrote furiously. "What color are his eyes?"

"I think they are bluish-gray, with a little brown in them."

"His hair?"

"Darkish — I couldn't really tell under all those coon tails."

"Coon tails? Do you suppose he killed them himself?"

"No. It looked more like one of those hats you get with cereal-box tops."

"Well, I won't say anything about it then — just coon-tail hat."

"Yeah, coon-tail hat's enough," I agreed. "And I think his shoes were just newspapers tied around his feet. That's good insulation, you know."

"Yeah?" Matt wrote that down.

"Did he say why he ran away?"

"I never asked him. Why does any boy run away?"

Matt put down his pencil and thought. "Well, I ran away once because I thought how sorry everybody would be when I was gone. How they'd cry and wish they'd been nicer to me." He laughed.

Then I said, "I ran away once because . . . well, because I wanted to do something else."

"That's a good reason," said Matt. "Do you suppose that's why . . . by the way, what is his name?"

"I never asked him," I said truthfully.

"What do you suppose he really eats and lives on?" asked Matt.

"Fish, roots, berries, nuts, rabbits. There's a lot of food around the woods if you look for it, I guess."

"Roots? Roots wouldn't be good."

"Well, carrots are roots."

"By golly, they are; and so are potatoes,

sort of. Fish?" pondered Matt, "I suppose there are lots of fish around here."

"The streams are full of them."

"You've really seen him, huh? He really is in these mountains?"

"Sure, I've seen him," I said. Finally I stood up.

"I gotta get home. I go the other way. You just follow this road to the town, and I think you can get a bus from there."

"Now wait," he said. "Let me read it back to you to check the details."

"Sure."

Matt stood up, blew on his hands and read: "The wild boy of the Catskills does exist. He has dark brown hair, black eyes, and wears a handsome deerskin suit that he apparently made himself. He is ruddy and in excellent health, and is able to build a fire with flint and steel as fast as a man can light a match.

"His actual dwelling is a secret, but his means of support is a beautiful falcon. The falcon flies off the boy's fist, and kills rabbits and pheasants when the boy needs food. He only takes what he needs. The boy's name is not known, but he ran away from home and never went back."

"No, Matt, no," I begged.

I was about to wrestle it out with him when he said furtively, "I'll make a deal with you. Let me spend my spring vacation with you, and I won't print a word of it. I'll write only what you've told me."

I looked at him and decided that it might be nice to have him. I said, "I'll meet you outside town any day you say, provided you let me blindfold you and lead you to my home, and provided you promise not to have a lot of photographers hiding in the woods. Do you know what would happen if you told on me?"

"Sure, the newsreels would roll up, the TV cameras would arrive, reporters would hang in the trees, and you'd be famous."

"Yes, and back in New York City."

"I'll write what you said and not even your mother will recognize you."

"Make it some other town, and it's a deal," I said. "You might say I am working for Civil Defense doing research by learning to live off the land. Tell them not to be afraid, that crayfish are delicious and caves are warm."

Matt liked that. He sat down again. "Tell me some of the plants and animals you eat, so that they will know what to do. We can make this informative."

I sat down and listed some of the better wild plants and the more easily obtainable mammals and fish. I gave him a few good recipes, and told him that I didn't recommend anyone trying to live off the land unless they liked oysters and spinach.

Matt liked that. He wrote and wrote. Finally he said, "My hands are cold. I'd better go. But I'll see you on April twelfth at three thirty outside of town. Okay? And just to prove that I'm a man of my word, I'll bring you a copy of what I write."

"Well, you better not give me away. I have a scout in civilization who follows all these stories."

We shook hands and he departed at a brisk pace.

I returned to my patch on the mountain, talking to myself all the way. I talk to myself a lot, but everyone does. The human being, even in the midst of people, spends nine tenths of his time alone with the private voices of his own head. Living alone on a mountain is not much different, except that your speaking voice gets rusty. I talked inside my head all the way home, thinking up schemes, holding conversations with Bando and Dad and Matt Spell. I worded the article for Matt after discussing it with Bando, and

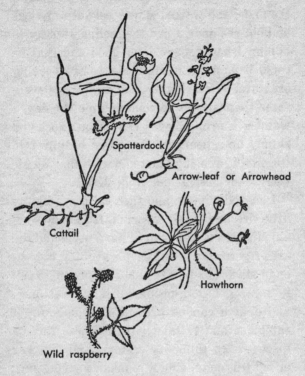

Spatterdock

Arrow-leaf or Arrowhead

Cattail

Hawthorn

Wild raspberry

made it sound very convincing without giving myself up. I kind of wanted to write it down and send it to Matt, but I didn't.

I entered my tree, tied Frightful to the bedpost, and there was Jessie Coon James. It had been months since I'd seen him. He was curled up on my bed, asleep. A turtle shell that had been full of cracked walnuts was empty beside him. He awoke, jumped to the floor, and walked slowly between my legs and out the door. I had the feeling Jessie was hoping I had departed for good and that he could have my den. He was a comfort-loving creature. I was bigger and my hands were freer than his, so he conceded me the den. I watched him climb over The Baron's rock and shinny up a hemlock. He moved heavily into the limbs, and it occurred to me that Jessie was a she-Jessie, not a he-Jessie.

I cooked supper, and then sat down by my little fire and called a forum. It is very sociable inside my head, and I have perfected the art of getting a lot of people arguing together in silence or in a forum, as I prefer to call it. I can get four people all talking at once, and a fifth can be present, but generally I can't get him to talk. Usually these forums discuss such things as a storm and whether or not it is coming, how to make a spring suit, and how to enlarge my house without destroying the life in the tree. Tonight, however, they discussed what to do about Matt Spell. Dad kept telling me to go right down to the city and make sure he published nothing, not even a made-up story. Bando said, "No, it's all right; he still doesn't know where you live." And then Matt walked into the conversation and said that he wanted to spend his spring vacation with me, and that he promised not to do anything untoward. Matt kept using "untoward" — I don't know where he got that expression, but he liked it and kept using it — that's how I knew Matt was speaking; everything was "untoward."

That night I fell asleep with all these people discussing the probability of my being found and hauled back to the city. Suddenly Frightful broke into the conversation. She said, "Don't let that Matt come up here. He eats too much." That was the first time that Frightful had ever talked in a forum. I was delighted, for I was always sure that she had more to say than a few cries. She had not missed Matt's appetite.

The forum dissolved in a good humor, everyone being delighted with Frightful. I lifted my head to look at her. She had her beak in the feathers of her back, sound asleep.

She spoke in my head, however, and said, "You really want to be found, or you would not have told Matt all you did."

"I like you better when you don't talk," I said, pulled the deer hide over me, and fell into a deep sleep.

In Which I Cooperate
With the Ending

By THE MIDDLE OF MARCH I could have told you it was spring without looking. Jessie did not come around any more. She was fishing the rewarding waters of the open stream; she was returning to a tree hollow full of babies. The Baron Weasel did not come by. There were salamanders and frogs to keep him busy. The chickadees sang alone, not in a winter group, and the skunks and minks and foxes found food more abundant in the forest than at my tree house. The circumstances that had brought us all together in the winter were no more. There was food on the land, and the snow was slipping away.

By April I was no longer living off my

storehouse. There were bulbs, tubers, and greens to be had. Meals were varied once more. There were frogs' legs, eggs, and turtle soup on my table.

I took my baths in the spring again, rather than in the turtle shell with warmed-over snow. I plunged regularly into the icy water of the spring, shouting as my breath was grabbed from my lungs. I scrubbed, ran for my tree. I dried myself before the fire, shouting as I stepped into my clothes. Then I would sing. I made up a lot of nice songs after my bath, one of which I taught to a man who was hiking along the top of the gorge one day.

He said his name was Aaron, and he was quiet and tall. I found him sitting on the edge of the cliff, looking across the valley. He was humming little tunes. He had a sad smile that never went away. I knew I would not have to hide from him just by looking at him, so I walked up and sat down beside him. I taught him my "cold-water song."

I learned he wrote songs and that he was from New York. He had come to the Catskills for the Passover festivities and had wandered off for the day. He was about to go back when I sat down and said, "I heard you humming."

"Yes," he said. "I hum a good deal. Can you hum?"

"Yes," I replied, "I can hum. I hum a good deal too, and even sing, especially when I get out of the spring in the morning. Then I really sing aloud."

"Let's hear you sing aloud."

So I said, feeling very relaxed with the sun shining on my head, "All right, I'll sing you my cold-water song."

"I like that," Aaron said. "Sing it again." So I did.

"Let me suggest a few changes." He changed a few words to fit the tune and the tune to fit the words, and then we both sang it.

"Mind if I use the hum-hum-hum dee-dee part?" he asked presently.

"You can use it all," I said. "Tunes are free up here. I got that from the red-eyed vireo."

He sat up and said, "What other songs are sung up here?"

I whistled him the "hi-chickadee" song of the black-capped Mr. Bracket and the waterfall song of the wood thrush. He took out a card, lined it with five lines, and wrote in little marks. I stretched back in the sun and hummed the song of the brown thrasher and of Barometer, the nuthatch. Then I boomed out the song of the great horned owl and stopped.

"That's enough, isn't it?" I asked.

"I guess so." He lay back and stretched, looked into the leaves, and said, "If I do something with this, I'll come back and play it to you. I'll bring my portable organ."

"Fine," I said.

Then, after a drowsy pause, he said, "Will you be around these parts this summer?"

"I'll be around," I said. Aaron fell asleep, and I rolled over in the sun. I liked him. He hadn't asked me one personal question. Oddly enough, I wasn't sure whether that made me glad or not. Then I thought of the words Frightful had spoken in my head, "You want to be found," and I began to wonder. I had sought out a human being. This would not have happened a year ago.

I fell asleep. When I awoke, Aaron was gone and Frightful was circling me. She saw me stir, swooped in, and sat on a rock beside me. I said "Hi," but did not get up, just lay still listening to the birds, the snips and sputs of insects moving in the dry leaves, and the air stirring the newly leafing trees. Nothing went on in my head. It was comfortably blank. I knew the pleasures of the lizard on the log who knows where his next meal is coming from. I also knew his boredom. After an hour I did have a thought. Aaron had said that he was up in the Catskills for Passover. Then it must also be near Easter, and Matt would be coming soon. I had not counted notches in weeks.

A cool shadow crossed my face and I arose, whistled for Frightful to come to my hand, and wandered slowly home, stuffing my pockets with spring beauty bulbs as I went.

Several days later I met Matt on Route 27 at three thirty. I tied his handkerchief around his eyes and led him, stumbling and tripping, up the mountain. I went almost directly home. I guess I didn't much care if he remembered how to get there or not. When I took off the blindfold, he looked around.

"Where are we? Where's your house?" I sat down and motioned him to sit. He did so with great willingness — in fact he flopped.

"What do you sleep on, the ground?"

I pointed to the deerskin flaps moving in the wind in the hemlock.

"Whatdaya do, live in a tree?"

"Yep." Matt bounced to his feet and we went in. I propped the door open so that the light streamed in, and he shouted with joy. I lit the tallow candle and we went over every-thing, and each invention he viewed with a shout.

While I prepared trout baked in wild grape leaves, Matt sat on the bed and told me the world news in brief. I listened with care to the trouble in Europe, the trouble in the Far East, the trouble in the South, and the trouble in America. Also to a few sensational murders, some ball scores, and his report card.

"It all proves my point," I said sagely. "People live too close together."

"Is that why you are here?"

"Well, not exactly. The main reason is that I don't like to be dependent, particularly on electricity, rails, steam, oil, coal, machines, and all those things that can go wrong."

"Well, is that why you are up here?"

"Well, not exactly. Some men climbed Mount Everest because it was there. Here is a wilderness."

"Is that why?"

"Aw, come on, Matt. See that falcon? Hear those white-throated sparrows? Smell that skunk? Well, the falcon takes the sky, the white-throated sparrow takes the low bushes, the skunk takes the earth, you take the newspaper office, I take the woods."

"Don't you get lonely?"

"Lonely? I've hardly had a quiet moment since arriving. Stop being a reporter and let's eat. Besides, there are people in the city who are lonelier than I."

"Okay. Let's eat. This is good — darned good — in fact the best meal I've ever eaten." He ate and stopped asking questions.

We spent the next week fishing, hunting, trapping, gathering greens and bulbs. Matt talked less and less, slept, hiked, and pondered. He also ate well, and kept Frightful very busy. He made himself a pair of moccasins out of deer hide, and a hat that I can't even describe. We didn't have a mirror, so he never knew how it looked, but I can say this: when I happened to meet him as we came fishing along a stream bed, I was always startled. I never did get used to that hat.

Toward the end of the week, who should we find sleeping in my bed after returning from a fishing trip but Bando! Spring vacation, he said. That night we played our reed whistles for Matt, by an outdoor fire. It was that warm. Matt and Bando also decided to make a guest house out of one of the other trees. I said "Yes, let's," because I felt that way, although I knew what it meant.

A guest house meant I was no longer a

runaway. I was no longer hiding in the wilderness. I was living in the woods like anyone else lives in a house. People drop by, neighbors come for dinner, there are three meals to get, the shopping to do, the cleaning to accomplish. I felt exactly as I felt when I was home. The only difference was that I was a little harder to visit out here, but not too hard. There sat Matt and Bando.

We all burned and dug out another hemlock. I worked with them, wondering what was happening to me. Why didn't I cry "No"? What made me happily build a city in the forest — because that is what we were doing.

When the tree was done, Bando had discovered that the sap was running in willow trees and the limbs were just right for slide whistles. He spent the evening making us trombones. We played them together. That word *together*. Maybe that was the answer to the city.

Matt said rather uncomfortably just before bedtime, "There may be some photographers in these hills."

"Matt!" I hardly protested. "What did you write?"

It was Bando who pulled out the article.

He read it, a few follow-ups, and comments

from many other papers. Then he leaned back against his leaning tree, as it had come to be, and puffed silently on his pipe.

"Let's face it, Thoreau, you can't live in America today and be quietly different. If you are going to be different, you are going to stand out, and people are going to hear about you; and in your case, if they hear about you, they will remove you to the city or move to you, and you won't be different any more." A pause.

"Did the owls nest, Thoreau?"

I told him about the owls and how the young played around the hemlock, and then we went to bed a little sad — all of us. Time was running out.

Matt had to return to school, and Bando stayed on to help burn out another tree for another guest house. We chopped off the blackened wood, made one bed, and started the second before he had to return to his teaching.

I wasn't alone long. Mr. Jacket found me.

I was out on the raft trying to catch an enormous snapping turtle. He would take my line, but when I got his head above water, he would eye me with those cold, ancient eyes and let go. Frightful was nearby. I was making a noose to throw over the turtle's head the next time it surfaced when Frightful lit on my shoulder with a thud and a hard grip. She was drawn up and tense, which in her language said "people," so I wasn't surprised to hear a voice call from across the stream, "Hi, Daniel Boone. What are you doing?" There stood Mr. Jacket.

"I am trying to get this whale of a snapper," I said in such an ordinary voice that it was dull.

I went on with the noose making, and he called to me, "Hit it with a club."

I still couldn't catch the old tiger, so I rafted to shore and got Mr. Jacket. About an hour later we had the turtle, had cleaned it, and I knew that Mr. Jacket was Tom Sidler.

"Come on up to the house," I said, and he came on up to the house, and it was just like after school on Third Avenue. He wanted to see everything of course, and he did think it unusual, but he got over it in a hurry and settled down to helping me prepare the meat for turtle soup.

He dug the onions for it while I got it boiling in a tin can. Turtle is as tough as rock, and has to be boiled for hours before it gets tender. We flavored the soup with hickory salt, and cut a lot of Solomon's-seal tubers into it. Tom said it was too thin, and I thickened it with mashed up nuts — I had run out of acorn flour. I tried some orris root in it — pretty fair.

"Wanta stay and eat it and spend the night?" I asked him somewhere along the way. He said "Sure," but added that he had better go home and tell his mother. It took him about two hours to get back, and the turtle was still tough, so we went out to the meadow to fly Frightful. She caught her own meal, we tied her to her perch, and climbed in the gorge until almost dark. We ate turtle soup. Tom slept in the guest tree.

I lay awake wondering what had happened. Everything seemed so everyday.

I liked Tom and he liked me, and he came up often, almost every weekend. He told me about his bowling team and some of his friends, and I began to feel I knew a lot of people in the town below the mountain. This made my wilderness small. When Tom left one weekend I wrote this down:

"Tom said that he and Reed went into an empty house, and when they heard the real-estate man come in, they slid down the laundry chute to the basement and crawled out the basement window. He said a water main broke and flooded the school grounds, and all the kids took off their shoes and played baseball in it."

I drew a line through all this and then I wrote:

"I haven't seen The Baron Weasel. I think he has deserted his den by the boulder. A catbird is nesting nearby. Apparently it has learned that Frightful is tied some of the time, because it comes right up to the fireplace for scraps when the leash is snapped."

I drew a line through this too, and filled up the rest of the piece of bark with a drawing of Frightful.

I went to the library the next day and took out four books.

Aaron came back. He came right to the hemlock forest and called. I didn't ask him how he knew I was there. He stayed a week, mostly puttering around with the willow whistles. He never asked what I was doing on the mountain. It was as if he already knew. As if he had talked to someone or read something, and there was nothing more to question. I had the feeling that I was an old story somewhere beyond the foot of the mountain. I didn't care.

Bando got a car, and he came up more often. He never mentioned any more newspaper stories, and I never asked him. I just said to him one day, "I seem to have an address now."

He said, "You do."

I said, "Is it Broadway and Forty-second Street?"

He said, "Almost." His eyebrows knitted and he looked at me sadly.

"It's all right, Bando. Maybe you'd better bring me a shirt and some blue jeans when you come next time. I was thinking, if they haven't sold that house in town, maybe Tom and I could slide down the laundry chute."

Bando slowly turned a willow whistle over in his hands. He didn't play it.

In Which the City Comes to Me

THE WARBLERS ARRIVED, the trees turned summer-green, and June burst over the mountain. It smelled good, tasted good, and was gentle to the eyes.

I was stretched out on the big rock in the meadow one morning. Frightful was jabbing at some insect in the grass below me when suddenly a flashbulb exploded and a man appeared.

"Wild boy!" he said, and took another picture. "What are you doing, eating nuts?"

I sat up. My heart was heavy. It was so heavy that I posed for him holding Frightful on my fist. I refused to take him to my tree, however, and he finally left. Two other photographers came, and a reporter. I talked a little. When they left, I rolled over on my stomach and wondered if I could get in touch with the Department of Interior and find out more about the public lands in the West. My next thought was the baseball game in the flooded school yard.

Four days passed, and I talked to many reporters and photographers. At noon of the fifth day a voice called from the glen: "I know you are there!"

"Dad!" I shouted, and once again burst down the mountainside to see my father.

As I ran toward him, I heard sounds that stopped me. The sound of branches and twigs breaking, of the flowers being crushed. Hordes were coming. For a long moment I stood wondering whether to meet Dad or run forever. I was self-sufficient; I could travel the world over, never needing a penny, never asking anything of anyone. I could cross to Asia in a canoe via the Bering Strait. I could raft to an island. I could go around the world on the fruits of the land. I started to run. I got as far as the gorge and turned back. I wanted to see Dad.

I walked down the mountain to greet him and to face the people he had brought from the city to photograph me, interview me, and bring me home. I walked slowly, knowing that it was all over. I could hear the voices of the other people. They filled my silent mountain.

Then I jumped in the air and laughed for joy. I recognized my four-year-old brother's pleasure song. The family! Dad had brought the family! Every one of them. I ran, twisting and turning through the trees like a Cooper's hawk, and occasionally riding a free fifty feet downhill on an aspen sapling.

"Dad! Mom!" I shouted as I came upon them along the stream bed, carefully picking their way through raspberry bushes. Dad gave me a resounding slap and Mother hugged me until she cried.

John jumped on me. Jim threw me into the rushes. Mary sat on me. Alice put leaves in my hair. Hank pulled Jim off. Joan pulled me to my feet, and Jake bit my ankle. That cute little baby sister toddled away from me and cried.

"Wow! All of New York!" I said proudly. "This is a great day for the Katerskills."

I led them proudly up the mountain, thinking about dinner and what I had that would go around. I knew how Mother felt when we brought in friends for dinner.

As we approached the hemlock grove, I noticed that Dad was carrying a pack. He explained it as food for the first few days, or until I could teach John, Jim, Hank, and Jake how to live off the land. I winked at him.

"But, Dad, a Gribley is not for the land."

"What do you mean?" he shouted. "The Gribleys have had land for three generations. We pioneer, we open the land." He was almost singing.

"And then we go to sea," I said.

"Things have changed. Child labor laws — you can't take children to sea."

I should have glowed over such a confession from Dad had I not been making furious plans as we climbed: food, beds, chores. Dad, however, had had since Christmas to outplan me. He strung up hammocks for everyone all through the forest, and you never heard a happier bunch of kids. The singing and shouting and giggling sent the birds and wildlife deeper into the shadows. Even little Nina had a hammock, and though she was only a toddler, she cooed and giggled all by herself as she rocked between two aspens near the meadow. We ate Mother's fried chicken. Chicken is good; it tastes like chicken.

I shall never forget that evening.

And I shall never forget what Dad said, "Son, when I told your mother where you were, she said, 'Well, if he doesn't want to come home, then we will bring home to him.' And that's why we are all here."

I was stunned. I was beginning to realize that this was not an overnight camping trip, but a permanent arrangement. Mother saw my expression and said, "When you are of age, you can go wherever you please. Until then, I still have to take care of you, according to all the law I can find." She put her arm around me, and we rocked ever so slightly. "Besides, I am not a Gribley. I am a Stuart, and the Stuarts loved the land." She looked at the mountain and the meadow and the gorge, and I felt her feet squeeze into the earth and take root.

The next day I took John, Jim, and Hank out into the mountain meadows with Frightful to see if we could not round up enough food to feed this city of people. We did pretty well.

When we came back, there was Dad with four four-by-fours, erected at the edge of my meadow, and a pile of wood that would have covered a barn.

"Gosh, Dad," I cried, "what on earth are you doing?"

"We are going to have a house," he said.

I was stunned and hurt.

"A house! You'll spoil everything!" I protested. "Can't we all live in trees and hammocks?"

"No. Your mother said that she was going to give you a decent home, and in her way of looking at it, that means a roof and doors. She got awfully mad at those newspaper stories inferring that she had not done her duty."

"But she did." I was almost at the point of tears. "She's a swell mother. What other boy has a mother who would let him do what I did?"

"I know, I know; but a woman lives among her neighbors. Your mother took all those editorials personally, as if they were Mr. Bracket and Mrs. O'Brien speaking. The nation became her neighbors, and no one, not even —" He hesitated. A catbird meowed. "Not even that catbird is going to think that she neglected you."

I was about to protest in a loud strong voice when Mother's arm slipped around my shoulder.

"That's how it is until you are eighteen, Sam," she said. And that ended it.